COLD SHOCK

"Nancy?" Frank said urgently, starting up from his chair. "Four guys in ski masks just came in."

Nancy whirled around. Two of the men were standing against the wall by the disco's exit door. The other two seemed to be doing nothing besides lazily checking out the club and bouncing a little to the music.

Suddenly John leaned down and whispered something to Bess. Bess nodded, and the two of them started toward the main exit.

They never got there. With silent efficiency, two of the masked men grabbed Bess from behind. Her eyes widened in shock. But she didn't have time to scream as they pulled her toward the wall.

Then the three of them melted into the darkness of an underground tunnel.

*NANCY DREW AND THE HARDY BOYS
TEAM UP
IN A BRAND-NEW ADVENTURE!*

D0090157

Nancy Drew & Hardy Boys SuperMysteries

DOUBLE CROSSING
A CRIME FOR CHRISTMAS

Available from ARCHWAY Paperbacks

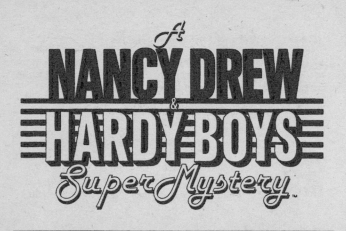

A NANCY DREW & HARDY BOYS Super Mystery

A CRIME FOR CHRISTMAS

Carolyn Keene

AN ARCHWAY PAPERBACK
Published by POCKET BOOKS
New York   London   Toronto   Sydney   Tokyo

AN ARCHWAY PAPERBACK *Original*

An Archway Paperback published by
POCKET BOOKS, a division of Simon & Schuster Inc.
1230 Avenue of the Americas, New York, NY 10020

ISBN: 0-671-64918-3

First Archway Paperback printing November 1988

10 9 8 7 6 5 4 3 2

NANCY DREW, THE HARDY BOYS, AN ARCHWAY
PAPERBACK and colophon are registered trademarks of
Simon & Schuster Inc.

NANCY DREW & HARDY BOYS SUPERMYSTERY
is a trademark of Simon & Schuster Inc.

Printed in the U.S.A.

IL 7+

A CRIME FOR CHRISTMAS

Chapter

One

JACK FROST ROASTING on an open fire; chestnuts nipping at your nose . . ." The cabdriver absentmindedly tapped the rhythm on his steering wheel as he sang. Outside the taxi, a loud chorus of car horns blared an unhappy accompaniment.

In the backseat, Nancy Drew was half listening as she watched a steady stream of Christmas shoppers bustle in and out of Saks Fifth Avenue. All at once she exchanged a puzzled frown with her friend Bess Marvin. Then she leaned forward, her blue eyes twinkling. "Wait a minute," she said to the cabdriver. "Those aren't the right words!"

The cabdriver grinned. "I thought you'd never notice," he said. "Most of my customers don't, you know. They're too busy getting mad about something or other. But, hey, it's Christmas, it's Fifth Avenue—and that means gridlock, right? You got to accept it and keep your sense of humor, know what I mean?"

"Sure," Nancy answered. She looked over at Bess, and both girls stifled a giggle.

"Atta girl! Say, you two are from out of town— right? You don't talk like New Yorkers."

Bess nodded. "We're from the Midwest," she said. "A place called River Heights."

"I got relatives in Chicago," the cabdriver answered. "Is that near River Heights?"

"Pretty near," Bess said.

As the cab crept along and Bess made small talk with the driver, Nancy began to grow impatient. There was a lot to do before she and Bess were to meet Frank and Joe Hardy that afternoon. She glanced out the window. The main door of Saks, which had been a few feet ahead of them ten minutes earlier, was now only a few feet behind them.

Tucking her reddish blond hair into her angora beret, Nancy rolled down her window and leaned out to get a view of the intersection ahead. A motorcade of long, black limousines was passing through it, blocking traffic from their direction.

Nancy pulled her head back in the taxi. The driver was still gabbing away. "I tell you, I've seen all kinds in the Big Apple—"

"Excuse me," Nancy interrupted. "There's a whole line of stretch limos up ahead. Do you know what's going on?"

The driver rolled down his window and craned his neck out to see up ahead. "Beats me," he said. "They've got diplomat license plates. Probably some sort of U.N. bigshots—" Suddenly he snapped his fingers. "I know! It must be that prince. What's his name? He was in the paper. You know, from that country—how do you say it—Sacone, Sacony? I think they're celebrating their five hundredth birthday or something."

Bess nudged Nancy in the ribs. "Sarconne!" she whispered excitedly.

Nancy nodded. Sarconne was the very reason she and Bess were in New York. Sam Peterson, the chief of police of New York City, had asked Frank and Joe Hardy to help him with a case that none of his people would be young enough to work on. Frank and Joe had then asked Nancy to help them.

"Yeah, that's it," the cabdriver said. "They're setting up some kind of exhibit at the Metropolitan Museum. The crown jewels, I think. Millions of bucks' worth of jewelry just sitting there— under glass!" He chuckled. "I bet every crook in town's got his eyes on those little trinkets."

He doesn't know how right he is, Nancy thought.

Her mind raced over the sketchy details of her new case, which, she knew, wasn't going to be easy. They didn't even know who they were looking for. "Two cat burglars" was all their sources could say. These two cat burglars, who dressed all in black, had pulled off several of the most spectacular thefts in New York City's history. Now, according to their sources, they were going after the Sarconne jewels.

Bess's eyes were shining. "I can't believe this. Crown Prince Jean-Claude may actually be riding in that car, only half a block in front of us!" She whipped out a compact from inside her purse and looked into the mirror. "Look at this!" she wailed. "My hair is a wreck."

She grabbed a comb and frantically began pulling it through her long blond hair. Nancy smiled. "Uh, Bess, I *don't* think he can see you," she said.

"I know, I know," Bess answered, lining her eyes with a matching blue pencil. "But what if our eyes meet by chance? What if he's staying at our hotel and we arrive together? Oh, I knew I shouldn't have eaten those pretzels. I can just hear what he's saying to his chauffeur. 'What eez zat *whale* doing in zee back of zat taxicab?'"

Nancy laughed. No matter how slim Bess was, she always felt she needed to lose five pounds. Nancy had heard her complain a million times, but never before with a French accent. "Look, Bess," she said, raising an eyebrow, "you *asked* to be involved in this case. Don't forget, we're not here to meet and date Prince Jean-Claude!"

"I know," Bess said with a sigh. "I'm sorry, but

4

he's got to be a hunk! I mean, he's young, he's a prince. Have you seen pictures of him?"

"Bess, you are amazing!"

Bess rolled her eyes and giggled. "Oh, please, Nancy, I'm half teasing." She gave Nancy a sweet, sincere look. "Of course, if the prince were to declare his love for me *after* we save his country's jewels . . ."

Bess glanced impishly at her friend, and Nancy scowled back at her—for about two seconds. Then they both broke into laughter.

The cabdriver shook his head. "I tell you, I've never seen two people so happy sitting in stopped traffic with the meter running."

Nancy's smile faded as she glanced at the dashboard and saw twenty dollars lit up in red on the meter. "Can't you take another route?" she asked the driver.

"All I can do is try," he answered. After the motorcade passed, he forced his way into the left lane and turned onto a side street and then eventually down Park Avenue.

"Okay, here we are!" he said when the meter had moved past twenty-four dollars.

Nancy and Bess turned and looked out the rear window. Up the center of Park Avenue, a line of small trees, twinkling with white Christmas lights, stretched into the distance. On their right, a sleek skyscraper loomed. Its forty-story twin towers disappeared into the slightly overcast winter sky.

Just as Nancy finished paying the fare, the taxi door swung open, and a doorman in a brown uniform leaned toward them. "Welcome to the Winslow," he said, extending his arm to Bess. Two porters reached into the open trunk of the taxi and heaved out all the luggage—one suitcase for Nancy and three for Bess.

Nancy and Bess followed the porters through the revolving glass and brass door into the grand lobby with its high, ornate gold-leaf ceiling. A fifteen-foot crystal chandelier cast a circular pattern of dappled light on the parquet floor. In the far right-hand corner of the lobby was a towering Christmas tree, and from a balcony above them "Silent Night," being played on a piano, drifted down.

Bess looked around in awe as she trailed Nancy to the registration desk. "*This* is the hotel the cat burglars use as their base of operations?" she asked.

"That's what our sources suspect," Nancy answered. "The Winslow is really upset about it. But what can they do? They have no idea *who* the burglars are—and they're afraid of bad publicity."

After they had registered, Bess and Nancy followed a bellboy through a marble arch to a bank of elevators with shining, sculpted brass doors. "But it will take us weeks to find these guys," Bess said. "Our room must be outrageously expensive!"

Nancy smiled. "The Winslow's putting us up

for free—Frank and Joe, too. Supposedly the younger burglar is about our age, so the Winslow management hopes we'll meet him and then figure out a way to stop him."

"What makes them so sure we'll be able to find these guys? I mean—there are practically no clues, right?"

Nancy nodded confidently. "Right. But those are the best kinds of mysteries."

Ding! The elevator door slid open, revealing an interior of oak-paneled walls. Bess sighed happily as she stepped inside and sat down on the built-in settee. "I do have one important question," she said. "Do you know if room service is included?"

Nancy and Bess pushed their way out of the revolving doors of Bloomingdale's, a large and elegant department store.

"I can't believe you talked me into buying all this stuff!" Nancy exclaimed, clutching a shiny red shopping bag that said "Christmas Mania at Bloomingdale's!" "I mean, I love shopping, but some of this stuff is just too much!"

Bess looked shocked. "You mean the *La Boue de Visage* European epidermal regeneration treatment? Nancy, that 'stuff' happens to be the rarest, most effective natural facial mask around. You can't get it back in River Heights!"

"I know," Nancy said. "But it still seems weird to pay so much for something that's really just mud dyed yellow."

7

"Remind me not to shop with you anymore. You're no fun," Bess teased.

Nancy looked at her watch. "I'll tell you what *would* be fun. We have about twenty minutes before we have to meet Frank and Joe. Let's walk over to Fifth Avenue and window-shop all the way. There are some fantastic stores on Fifty-seventh Street, and the displays will be great this time of year."

"You've finally come to your senses!" Bess said, moving forward excitedly. "There's a *gorgeous* jumpsuit I saw advertised in—"

Suddenly Bess stopped short, her face absolutely blank.

"Bess, what is it?" Nancy asked worriedly. "Bess?"

"I—I can't move," Bess said.

Nancy's face was taut with concern. "What's the matter? Are you all right?"

"That has to be the most fabulous smell in the world," Bess said in a hushed, almost reverent voice.

Nancy sniffed. The intoxicating aroma of chocolate hung heavy in the wintry air. She looked around the corner to her left to see an elegant little shop called Chocolate Revelations.

"I think we should skip the window-shopping," Bess said.

Nancy gave her a knowing glance. "This *is* an emergency!" And she tore around the corner and into the shop, Bess at her heels.

Inside, the aroma was almost overpowering. A

hand-painted sign proclaimed: All Chocolates Made on the Premises. Customers were lined up to buy the special of the day, small wooden boxes of candy tied up in red, green, and gold ribbon. "Everything looks wonderful! Bess, what are you going to get?" Nancy asked, peering over the shoulder of the woman in front of her.

Bess didn't answer. Nancy looked around and spotted her at the far end of the store, smiling wide-eyed across the glass counter.

Nancy grinned. Leave it to Bess to find the only tall, muscular, blond-haired salesperson in the store.

"Nancy, meet Tony," Bess said as Nancy walked up. "I just asked him to get me one of those incredible creations on that tray in there!" She pointed toward an open door behind Tony.

Nancy looked into the back room, which was filled with candy-making equipment. There she saw a huge metal tray covered with rows of intricately molded chocolate crowns.

Tony nodded hello to Nancy. Then he turned to Bess with a dimpled smile. "Sorry, those aren't for sale. I'm supposed to put them in a box. They're a special order. We have to work every evening until Christmas to handle all the special orders we get this time of year."

Bess put on a weak smile. "That's okay, Tony," she said, trying not to let her disappointment show.

"Let's get something else then," Nancy suggested.

Tony looked quickly right and then left. "Hang on a second," he said with a mischievous grin. He sneaked into the back room and brought out a small square wooden box. "Don't tell anybody," he whispered, winking at Bess. "It's on me."

Bess smiled radiantly as Tony slipped the box into a shopping bag. "Merry Christmas!" he whispered, handing it over.

"Oh, thank you *so* much, Tony," she gushed.

Nancy put her arm through Bess's and gently pulled her away. "Let's go. It's getting late."

The two girls squeezed past the other customers and made their way outside and over to Fifth Avenue. They looked up to see a huge, elaborate snowflake, made of small lights, glowing above the intersection of Fifth and Fifty-seventh.

"This is it," Nancy said, glancing at the street sign.

Exhausted, Bess surveyed all four street corners. "Where are Frank and Joe? I mean, we ran all this way and— *Hey!* My chocolate crown!"

"What happened, Bess? Did you leave it—"

"No!" Bess cried, her eyes blazing. "That guy just stole it out of my hand! Stop! Thief!"

Chapter

Two

Nancy whipped around—and saw three men deftly weaving through the crowd. She thrust her shopping bag into Bess's arms and raced after them.

The trio quickly disappeared into the throng of shoppers. Nancy began sidestepping people as she ran. I'll never get to them through these crowds! she thought. But surprisingly she caught a glimpse of two of the men standing on Fifty-sixth Street. Both were wearing hats pulled low and were casting quick glances up and down the street. The one on the left was clutching Bess's shopping bag.

Nancy charged the man on the left and grabbed the arm that was holding the shopping bag. She yanked it behind his back and kicked him sharply behind the knees.

"Ow!" the man cried out, collapsing onto the ground.

All around them, shoppers gasped.

There was a moment of stunned silence before the man on the sidewalk peered up. For the first time Nancy got a good look at his face.

Nancy's jaw dropped. "Joe Hardy!" she exclaimed. She looked over and saw Frank Hardy watching them, doubled over with laughter. "That was a mean trick. I thought you were——"

"The infamous New York City chocolate thieves?" Frank said.

He was grinning as he extended his hand to Joe.

"Everything's all right, everybody," Nancy said to the bewildered shoppers. They slowly began to disperse.

Joe quickly brushed off his brown leather bomber jacket and pushed a lock of wavy blond hair away off his forehead. "I'd hate to see what you do to real bad guys," he grumbled.

Frank Hardy chuckled. "I don't know, Joe," he said. "I think you've met your match." He smiled at Nancy, and her cheeks reddened.

Joe looked insulted. "Hey, what do you mean, my *match?* My back was to her——"

At that moment a breathless voice cut Joe off.

"Oh! There you are! Did you find those rotten—"

Nancy, Frank, and Joe turned to see Bess. She was struggling toward them loaded down with shopping bags.

"Here they are, Bess," Nancy said. "The chocolate-nappers."

Bess stared disbelievingly at the two boys. "What was this—a joke? How could you?"

"No!" Frank exclaimed, disbelieving. "*We* didn't take your bag. We were crossing the street to meet you when we saw the whole thing happen."

Joe nodded. "The guy got away, but he knocked into someone and the bag fell onto the ground." He shrugged. "Probably some shoplifter with a sweet tooth."

"Well, this was some welcome to New York City," Nancy said.

Joe rolled his eyes. "Hope it's not a prediction of the way this whole case is going to go."

Frank reached over and grabbed some of Bess's shopping bags. "I say we forget about it and stick to our dinner plans. The Hard Rock Café is very near."

"Great idea!" Bess replied. "I'm starving."

As the four of them walked back up to Fifty-seventh Street, Nancy and Frank led the way.

"I hope this place is good," Frank said. "I'm starving."

"Yeah," Nancy said. "Me, too."

13

Inside she cringed. Yeah. Me, too. Was that all she could say to him? For some reason she was starting to feel nervous.

Maybe there was something about Frank. Maybe it was his deep brown eyes, which sparkled whenever he spoke to her. Maybe it was his keen intelligence, which kept questioning her.

Whatever it was, Nancy felt a strange confusion. Being with Frank made her feel excited and alive, but also she felt slightly guilty about her boyfriend, Ned Nickerson.

Nancy laughed at herself. After all, it wasn't as if she were in *love* with Frank. It was so ridiculous to have guilt pangs! Nobody could make her lose her love for Ned. At least she'd never *known* anyone who could . . .

Lost in thought, she suddenly became aware of Frank's voice. "Hello! Earth to Nancy!" he was saying.

Nancy looked over to see him smiling quizzically at her. "Oh, sorry," she answered. "I was just—just thinking about the case, that's all. We have a lot of work to do."

Frank nodded. "I know. Joe brought along our notes. We can talk about them over dinner." He tossed a glance over his shoulder at his brother. "That is, *if* we can tear him away from Bess."

Nancy looked back to see an animated Joe talking and gesturing wildly. Bess was gazing up at him, a broad smile on her face.

"Oh, no," Nancy groaned.

"What?" asked Frank.

"Never mind." She looked up. "Hey, this looks like the place!"

Sticking out of a nearby building was the back end of a shiny black Cadillac from the 1960s. It looked as if it had passed right through the wall and now was stuck there. Below it was a glass door that said Hard Rock Café.

As they walked through the door, the blare of rock music accosted them. Just inside, a crowd of people was gathered at the bar, and behind them waiters were racing back and forth between the kitchen and the tables.

A stunning, dark-skinned woman whisked out in front of them. "Right this way," she said in a harried voice.

The four friends followed her to the back of the restaurant, where a noisy table of twelve was finishing up dinner. The hostess placed four menus on a small table right next to the party. "Enjoy your meal," she said.

There was a burst of laughter from the big table. "Is this too loud?" Nancy asked the other three as she sat down. Both Frank and Joe shook their heads no, but Bess didn't answer. She was staring at the other table.

"Bess?" Nancy said. "Is this table okay?"

"Sorry," Bess said with a start. "It's fine."

Nancy looked at her menu. Underneath a few fancy-sounding entrees was the one thing she was absolutely dying for: a bacon cheeseburger deluxe. She glanced up and watched Joe and Bess sharing a menu.

15

"What's a braised endive?" Bess was saying.

Joe rubbed his chin thoughtfully for a second. "I'm not sure, but I believe it's a small plant that grows in the crevices of New York City sidewalks."

"Ugh, please!" Bess replied. She checked her menu again. "How about a free-range chicken?"

Joe put on a mock-serious expression. "I think those are what eat the braised endives," he said.

Nancy and Frank both rolled their eyes to the ceiling.

Soon a waiter took their orders, and after he'd walked away, Frank leaned forward on his elbows.

"Now," he said, "let's go over what we have so far on this case—which isn't very much. All we know about the burglars is they're masters of disguise. They've pulled off being male, female, young, old, Irish, Greek—you name it. But the police seem pretty sure that one of them is middle-aged and the other is about our age—but even this isn't definite. The definite lead we have is that they use the Winslow as a base. So, for starters, the best we can do is keep our eyes open for any suspicious-acting father-and-son teams."

"We'll need a photographer to stake out the lobby," Nancy suggested. "Someone who's good at sneaking photos."

"That's me!" Joe spoke up. "I've got the tourist act down pat. You know, snapping photos of the interior architecture, the flower arrangements"—he smiled—"and suspicious father-son teams."

"Great," Frank said. "We've got to find and stop these guys fast. Today's Tuesday, and the big Sarconne celebration at the U.N. is on Friday. The crown jewels are going to be on display at the party and before and after the party at the Metropolitan Museum. It's an international celebration of the country's five hundredth anniversary, and all kinds of dignitaries are going to be there—including the crown prince and his entourage."

"I'm sure there'll be tons of security," Nancy remarked.

"There will be—but that's exactly the kind of challenge these cat burglars seem to thrive on. . . ."

As Frank continued talking, Nancy glanced over at Bess again. Bess was trying to pay attention, but her eyes kept darting over to the table of twelve next to them.

Maybe the noise *is* distracting, Nancy thought. She looked over at the large party. They were all sitting now, and it seemed as if six or seven loud conversations were flying back and forth across the table at once. Everyone was screaming and gesturing—except one person.

He was wearing narrow sunglasses and was sitting sideways to the table, as if he didn't really want to be there. His turquoise shirt draped over a pair of broad, athletic shoulders and hung down casually over his jeans. A lock of brown hair fell across his forehead as he flashed a half grin in their direction. And when he took off his sunglasses, his luminous dark eyes shone directly at Bess.

Immediately Nancy felt uneasy. This was *exactly* the kind of guy who could sweep Bess off her feet. Not only was he good-looking, but there was a kind of glow about him—an incredible air of self-confidence and calm, as if nothing in the world ever fazed him.

Bess looked ready to be swept. She was returning his grin with a beaming smile of her own.

Under the table, Nancy gave Bess's leg a gentle kick. Bess jumped, blushed, and turned back to her friends.

"Experts at infiltration," Frank was saying. "They seem to get access to the most detailed information—maybe bribing or even posing as guards. One morning last April, the staff of Lussier Jewelers on Fifth Avenue walked in to find their entire precious stone collection gone."

Suddenly something out of the corner of her eye caught Nancy's attention. The guy at the next table was starting to leave. But before he walked off, he gave Bess a big wink. And from the blush on Bess's face, Nancy could tell she'd noticed it.

I hope this isn't going to get out of hand, Nancy thought gloomily. I need all the help I can get on this case.

* * *

"Okay, Joe and I are in room five eighty-three," Frank said as the four of them walked into the Winslow after dinner. From a lounge somewhere off the main lobby, a voice singing Christmas carols wafted into the lobby. "You're in . . . ?"

"Four thirty-two," Nancy replied.

"It's still early," Bess protested. "Let's not go up to our rooms yet. The night has just begun! Come on, let's go hear that singer and have some dessert!"

Nancy looked over toward the elevators. "I don't know," she said. "We really need to get started on this, and there's a lot of stuff we should check out in Frank's notes . . ."

"We can do that later and all day tomorrow," Bess pleaded. "Just a few minutes—"

A smooth, low-pitched voice interrupted her. "I hear the singer is one of the best in New York."

They all spun around and were face to face with the guy Nancy and Bess had noticed in the Hard Rock Café.

"Why don't you all come with me?" he said with a slight accent that Nancy couldn't quite place. "As my guests!"

For a moment no one knew what to say. Finally Joe spoke up. "Thanks for the offer. But do we know you?"

The guy smiled, his piercing brown eyes glittering and reflecting back the many lights of the crystal chandelier. "Sorry," he said with a chuckle. "My name is John. I was just thinking how strange it was seeing you all here. We *were* sitting next to one another at the Hard Rock Café, you know."

"John," Bess repeated dreamily. "I think I remember seeing you."

The dimples in John's cheeks deepened as he turned his attention to Bess.

"I'm Bess Marvin," she said quickly. "And these are my friends Nancy Drew and Frank and Joe Hardy. We're all staying here."

"I am, too," John said simply. "So you have no place to rush off to."

"Well, actually we do have some plans for the evening, John," Nancy said. "But thanks for inviting us."

"Just for a little while," John insisted. "One or two songs—"

He broke off suddenly and stared at a spot just behind Nancy. For a split second, Nancy thought fear played across his face.

Before any of them could reply, John said, "I shouldn't be bothering you. I do completely understand if you have other plans. Anyway, I'm certain we'll meet again very soon." With that, he turned and walked toward the bank of elevators.

"What was *that* all about?" asked Frank.

Nancy had turned to glance in the direction John had been looking. All she had seen were a couple of men moving into the lobby from the front door. She shrugged. Then, with a smile, she said, "I think Bess has an admirer."

Bess blushed as they all trooped to the elevator.

"Looks that way," Joe said, setting down one of Bess's bags to press the Up button. "Probably some actor. What a fake accent, huh?"

"I don't know, I thought it was pretty cute," Bess said, stepping inside the wood-paneled car.

Nancy and Bess got out on the fourth floor. "We'll drop off our stuff and meet you in a few minutes," Nancy called back to the boys.

Bess burst into their room. She twirled around once, dropped her shopping bags, and fell flat on her back on the bed. "I can't believe he's staying at the same hotel!" she gasped. "Did you notice his eyes, Nan?"

Nancy closed the door, shaking her head. It was going to be very tough to keep Bess's attention on the case.

"I mean, you have to admit he is adorable," Bess continued.

Nancy turned around to respond, but all that came out of her mouth was a gasp.

"Nan?" Bess said, sitting up. "What is it?"

A rattling noise at the window was the only reply. Bess turned toward it—and let out a strangled scream.

Silhouetted in the window beside her was the dark figure of a man—outside!

Chapter

Three

INSTANTLY NANCY REACHED for the light switch. With a click, the room fell into darkness. "Down behind the bed!" Nancy whispered.

She reached for the hotel phone and felt for the buttons in the dark. She punched Frank and Joe's number.

"Hello?" came Joe's voice.

"It's Nancy," she whispered. "Drop everything and come down here *now*—and hurry. Don't ask questions."

She hung up the phone and braced herself.

"Hello?" came a voice from the person outside the window. "Is everything all right in there?"

For a moment Nancy stared in disbelief as the

man reached above the window to pull himself up to the next floor. "Sorry if I scared you," he continued. "Just passing by."

There was no question about it. The voice was unmistakable.

"John!" Nancy said, flinging open the window. "What are you doing out there?"

John looked surprised as he peered into the darkened room. "You're Bess's friend—Nancy, right?"

"It *is* John," came Bess's excited voice.

Nancy could hear Bess scramble out from behind the bed and stumble across the carpeted floor to flick on the light switch.

Bess rushed to the window. "John, what—"

"Hello, Bess," John said. "Well, uh, this must seem very—*strange!*"

"You might say that," Nancy said.

John shook his head and looked uncomfortable as he climbed in through the window and rubbed his hands to warm them. "I don't blame you. I told myself no person in his right mind would try this! But it's just that—I don't know—after a couple of days in the city, I feel trapped. I long for the outdoors."

"So you climb buildings," Nancy said dryly.

"Right." John struggled for words. "You see—"

Whack-whack-whack! The knocking at the door sounded like gunshots.

"Open up, Nancy! What's going on in there?" came Frank's voice.

Nancy ran to the door. "It's all right, Frank," she said, pulling the door open. "False alarm. We had a surprise visitor—through our window. You remember John, don't you, guys?"

Joe looked astonished. He walked across the room staring at John, who grinned back at him. He inspected the window, and his eyes grew wider. "This window doesn't have a fire escape! How did you get up here?"

"I was about to explain that to Nancy and Bess," John said. "You see, I grew up in a place that is surrounded by great, thick forests and towering mountains, so I developed a passion for climbing! If this were a park, I'd be climbing trees. If it were a quarry, I'd be climbing rocks." He shrugged. "But it's the city, so I must settle for what I can find. I have to say, though, that this building's architect must have been an outdoorsman, too. The handholds on this building are wonderful!"

"Weren't you freezing out there?" Bess asked.

"Well—yes, I was. It is good to be indoors again."

John flashed a deep, dimpled smile. His dark, wavy hair had fallen just above his brown eyes, which seemed to glow like twin stars.

Even though John's story was hard to believe, Nancy did believe it. Also she could understand what Bess saw in him. He had a wild, carefree sparkle that was irresistible.

Bess was looking up at him with an admiring grin. "You're absolutely crazy!" she said.

John laughed. "Well, sometimes that's the best way to be! At least I'm never bored—nor boring, I hope."

Bess reached for the telephone. "Let me call room service and order you some hot chocolate or something."

"No!" John said it so forcefully that Bess pulled her hand back as if the phone were on fire. "Actually, I was thinking it might be more fun to warm ourselves up in a slightly livelier place. I know of a really hot downtown club—"

"Just a minute!" Frank protested. "We told you we had plans."

"But I insist!" John said. "Nancy and Bess may have just saved my life. I must repay them some way."

"I don't know about the rest of you," Bess said, "but I want to go. I mean, we're in New York City! It's Christmastime! Why stay cooped up in a stuffy old hotel? At least we can have fun *one* night!"

Nancy could tell that Bess had made up her mind to go. She looked over at John. There was something very charming about him—but also something very strange. What kind of person climbed the side of a hotel because he longed for the outdoors? They knew nothing about him— not even his last name!

The last thing Nancy wanted to do was let Bess go off alone in New York City with this guy. "I guess I'll go, too," she said.

Frank and Joe exchanged reluctant glances.

"Okay," Frank finally said. He looked at his watch. "It's nine forty-five. Let's be back by midnight. All right? We're going to need our rest."

The lights of Club Neon flashed across Nancy's eyes in a blur, and under her feet the transparent dance floor pulsed with color—first red, then green. The whole wall in front of her was lined with video monitors, and the air around her was filled with fake snow, being shot out of hidden ceiling pipes. Nancy smiled at Frank, who was dancing with her. "Christmas—club-style!" she said.

A few feet away Joe and Bess were dancing. Nancy leaned over to them. "We'll have to get going after this song," she called. "It's quarter to twelve."

"Oh, can't we just—" Bess began just as John walked up to her and Joe. He gave Joe an old-fashioned bow. "May I cut in?" he asked.

Somehow, what would have looked affected in most people seemed perfectly natural for John—even in a funky club like this. Turning toward him, Bess curtsied.

Joe stopped dancing abruptly and stalked away.

"Poor Bess," Frank said with a wry smile. "How is she going to choose between them?"

Nancy laughed. "Don't worry. It's her favorite kind of problem."

The music was getting louder now, and Nancy

and Frank threw themselves into the dance—until a voice beside them startled them out of their rhythm.

"Next stop, Laff Riot!"

They whirled around to face John. Over one arm he was carrying all their coats and with the other he had made a crook, which Bess was holding on to.

"Where are you going?" Nancy exclaimed.

"Time to move on!" John answered, handing Frank the coats. "This is the very best time for a comedy club! Come on!" He and Bess ran to the door.

"The guy is a little too much," Frank muttered.

Nancy nodded. "But he knows how to get his way." She indicated the bar clock with her eyes. "Don't forget, we were supposed to be back by midnight."

Before Frank could answer, Joe ran up to them. "What's going on?" he asked.

"We were just trying to figure that out ourselves," Frank replied.

Nancy and Frank shrugged together. "Well, I hear Laff Riot is great," Nancy said, giving in.

"Let's go after them!" Joe said. "We can't leave that guy alone with Bess."

"So I pitched a tent in Central Park, and I woke up to find a squirrel going through my wallet!" The comedian looked out into the audience and lifted his shoulders helplessly.

Joe was feeling restless. The crowd was chuckling, but he couldn't join in. The guy just wasn't funny to him. He looked around the room. Bess and Nancy were laughing politely, and Frank was looking at his watch. John had walked to the back, probably to get some refreshments.

No, it wasn't to get refreshments, Joe realized. He squinted to get a better view through the dark, smoke-filled room. John was almost hidden in a corner, talking to a man in a dark, full-length overcoat. The man was nodding solemnly.

Suddenly Joe was aware of a ripple of laughter around him. He jerked as Bess tugged on his elbow.

"Uh, yes, sir, the doors *are* locked, but the ticket taker *will* accept a reasonable bribe for your release," came the comedian's voice.

Joe swung around to see the comedian staring straight at him. He felt his face turn red as he realized that everyone was staring and laughing at *him!*

The comedian adjusted his horn-rimmed glasses. "I get this response a lot. The auto-escape reflex." He imitated a panicking person looking for an exit.

Joe could hear his brother trying to stifle a laugh. He sank back into his seat and listened to the rest of the comedian's monologue.

But within seconds he heard someone "aheming" at them from the entrance to the club—John.

"This guy is too much!" Joe said incredulously.

"Who?" Bess asked.

"John," Joe replied. "He wants us to leave now."

Bess and Nancy turned to look.

"Come on!" Bess said excitedly, and both girls got up to leave.

Frank and Joe could do nothing but follow. Outside John had flagged down a taxi. He opened the door for Bess and leaned into the driver's window. "The Winslow," he said.

"What?" Bess sputtered.

"Go ahead before he changes his mind," Nancy urged. "It's getting late."

Bess climbed in reluctantly, and Nancy followed her. Holding the door open, John turned to Frank and Joe. "Why didn't you tell me it was so late?" he asked. "I had promised to get you back much earlier. I'm so sorry."

The brothers exchanged a baffled glance as they climbed into the taxi.

"I'll meet you back at the hotel," John said. "I left my scarf inside."

"We'll wait," Bess said quickly.

"No, go on. I don't want to hold you. Anyway, I wouldn't fit in the cab." John slammed the door and ran back into the club.

Frank raised his eyebrows. "Very strange," he said.

The taxi pulled away from the curb, and Bess

let out a loud sigh. "*This* is what I always thought New York would be like. What a guy!"

Joe crossed his arms in front of him. "What a phony!"

Bess turned to glare at Joe. "Now, listen, Joe—"

But Joe cut her off. "I saw something very suspicious in the club. Remember when John got up and left for a few minutes? Well, I saw him, and he was in a deep conversation with a pretty sinister-looking older guy."

"So what?" Bess said. "It could have been anyone—the club owner, a stranger he just met. . . ."

"A stranger wearing a winter coat indoors and writing down what John was saying?" Joe answered. "Look, I know this guy's a lot of fun, but I just don't trust him. He never talks about himself, and have you noticed his eyes whenever we're in a public place?"

Frank nodded. "Always moving, as if—"

"As if he's being chased." Nancy finished Frank's sentence perfectly.

"Right," Joe continued. "Think about it. What kind of person just *happens* to climb the outside of a building in the night and has a clandestine meeting with an older man in the back of a club?"

Frank and Nancy caught on at the same time. Nancy gasped and Frank let out a low whistle.

"What! Will someone please fill me in?" Bess demanded.

Nancy gave her friend a troubled look. "Bess, those are things a young cat burglar might do."

Joe looked at the others matter-of-factly. "It is possible. He *is* the right age. I think we ought to keep an eye on him. If he's on to us, it could be big trouble."

Bess didn't say a word as she and Nancy walked down the hall to their room. Nancy half wanted to comfort her, to tell her that Joe was wrong. But what if John *was* one of the cat burglars? What exactly did he want with Bess? Was he going to use her in a crime? And what if Bess really did fall in love with him—would Nancy still be able to trust her on the case?

Nancy's mind was so filled with questions and doubts that she couldn't say anything to Bess. She stood back as Bess took out their computer encoded room card key. With a self-pitying sigh, Bess thrust the card in the slot, pushed the door open, turned on the foyer light—and screamed.

"No!" Bess shrieked.

Chapter

Four

NANCY RUSHED TO her friend's side and looked in. Her jaw fell open.

The covers had been torn off the beds. Clothes, sheets, and towels were strewn all over the floor. The girls' shopping bags lay in shreds by the wall, their contents dumped in a heap.

"Bess," Nancy said grimly, "something tells me we're very deeply into this case already."

Bess exhaled shakily. "I don't *like* being so involved in a case," she said. She walked over to the pile of merchandise on the floor. "All our Christmas shopping! I wonder if—" She reached down to sift through the pile.

"Don't touch anything!" Nancy said quickly. She reached for the telephone. "I have to call security first."

"Okay, ladies, we'll have our men work on it." The head of security for the Winslow scratched his head. "But I have to tell you, you're lucky nothing was stolen."

"I know we are," Nancy said soberly. "But it's more than luck. It's weird."

Frank was looking around the devastated room, trying to pick up clues. "You're sure you had nothing of value in here?" he said.

"*I* did," Bess answered. She opened a small jewelry box in the drawer of her night table and held up some gold earrings and a necklace. "They didn't touch these—and they're pretty expensive."

"You're lucky," the security guard said again. "The drawer was open, too. Maybe they just didn't think they could get enough for that jewelry. Some of these guys are only after the big stuff." He made a note in his pad and walked to the door. "Now, you make sure and call us if anything happens."

"Big help," Bess muttered as he walked out. She handed the jewelry box to Frank. "Here, why don't you keep this in your room, just in case?"

"Okay," Frank replied. "I think Joe accidentally carried two of your shopping bags to our room after supper. I'll put it with those."

Bess's eyes lit up. "One of those bags has my chocolate crown in it. Would you please bring it down here?"

"No problem," Joe said. He placed the last pillow back on the bed, surveyed the straightened room, and headed for the door. "I'll be back in a few minutes."

As soon as Frank and Joe had left, Bess plopped herself down on the bed and began to brush her hair. She didn't say a word as Nancy put on her pajamas and got ready for bed.

After making sure the windows were locked tight, Nancy slipped into one of the queen-size beds. Bess was sitting motionless on her own bed. With a yawn, Nancy said, "Aren't you going to get ready, Bess?"

"I guess," Bess answered dully.

"What's up? You scared of someone breaking in again?"

"No."

"Just wound up from our busy night?"

"No."

A tense silence fell over the room. Nancy sat up and looked her friend straight in the eye. "You're mad at me, right?"

Bess turned away. "Well, no. Not *mad*, Nancy. It's just that"—she exhaled with frustration—"I think you guys are being unfair to John. I mean, you're just assuming he's a criminal."

"I'm sorry, Bess," Nancy said sympathetically. She propped up her pillows and leaned back against the headboard. "I know how much you like John, but we have to be careful."

"I don't know, Nancy," Bess answered. "To tell you the truth, I think Joe has—*other* reasons for saying bad things about John."

"What do you mean?"

"Well, Joe's a nice guy and all, but haven't you noticed how weird he gets when John's around? I don't think he'd be this way if John weren't so charming and good-looking. I guess what I'm saying is, I think Joe might be a little mad that John's stealing all our attention."

"All *yours,* you mean," Nancy said with a knowing smile.

"Well, you know what I'm saying," Bess answered sheepishly.

Nancy laughed. "Maybe you're right, Bess. But Joe is a great detective, too. I've worked with him, and I know how professional he is. If he's suspicious about somebody, there's a good reason. And his theory *does* make sense."

Just then there was a knock at the door. "Your bags, ma'am!" Joe's voice said.

Nancy jumped out of bed, put on her robe, and went to the door. "Thanks, Joe," she said, carrying the shopping bags into the room.

Joe followed her and looked at both girls very seriously. "You call us at the slightest strange sound, all right? Especially if you have any unexpected visitors through the window!"

"Right," Nancy answered, smiling at Joe's big-brother routine.

"Okay, then. Good night," Joe said.

As the door shut, Bess sighed. "You know, Nancy, I realize that John acts a little strange. But you have to understand—to him, all that stuff he does probably seems absolutely normal. Maybe he's just one of those people who doesn't follow the crowd. Besides, he's too nice to be a cat burglar."

"We don't really know him at all. Why do you think he insisted that we go out tonight—and then kept us out longer than we'd agreed to stay? What if he wanted to clear us out so his partner could go to work in our room?"

Bess shook her head vehemently. "Nancy, that's ridiculous! I mean, even if it were all true, why would any cat burglar go to such trouble to rob *us?* We have nothing really valuable."

Nancy sighed—Bess had a point. "Yeah, you're right. I guess we're all grasping at straws." She flopped down onto her bed. "Let's just try to get some sleep, okay? Maybe we'll see things clearer in the morning."

"Okay," Bess said, reaching into her suitcase for her toothbrush. "Good night."

Nancy lay back down. She hoped she'd eased the tension between them. But she couldn't help noticing a chill in the air as Bess bustled around to get ready for bed.

As Nancy walked into the lobby, she looked up. On the balcony, amid the tables set up for late lunch, a pianist was playing "Jingle Bells" as Santa Claus strolled around and talked to the enthralled children.

"Nancy!" she heard behind her. She turned around to face Frank.

"Hi!" Nancy said. "What did you find out from security?"

The two of them walked over to an alcove beside the giant Christmas tree. "Nothing. I have a feeling we're not going to get much from them," Frank answered. "Anything from your end?"

"No. I talked to the cleaning staff and the porters. They weren't around at the time, and I can't find any clues in the hallways or stairwells." She shrugged. "It's a blank slate, Frank."

Frank smiled slightly. "Those are the best kind."

Nancy smiled. That sounded like something she would say.

"Where's Bess?" Frank asked.

"Spending the afternoon with John. I don't like it, but what could I say?" she asked. "Where's Joe?"

"He said he was going to hang out in the lobby and take pictures," said Frank. He looked around. "There he is."

On the other side of the lobby, Joe was snapping pictures with a telephoto lens.

"Let's stay back," Frank warned. "He looks as though he's on to something. I don't want to draw attention to him."

They slid behind the Christmas tree and watched as Joe moved quietly around. He seemed to have noticed something suspicious in the balcony café.

"What's he looking at?" Nancy asked.

"Can't tell," Frank answered.

Joe began moving the camera slowly to the right as he aimed through the viewfinder. Frank and Nancy followed his gaze up to the café, where a gorgeous auburn-haired girl was sitting at a small table, sipping something steaming hot from a patterned fine china cup.

Frank groaned. "I don't believe this!" he said.

Joe focused carefully and snapped.

The girl tossed back her hair and looked out over the lobby. She seemed to be admiring the Christmas decorations. Her face had a radiant smile—until she saw Joe.

Instantly Joe pulled the camera down and looked away, whistling.

"Smooth," Frank said sarcastically under his breath.

Frank and Nancy watched as the girl strode down the side stairs and across the lobby toward Joe. A wry smile creased her lips.

"Let's go over there," Frank murmured. "I've got to hear this." He strolled casually toward Joe, Nancy following. Joe looked a little startled when he saw them, but he gave no sign of recognition.

The auburn-haired girl walked right up behind Joe and watched for a moment as he studied the

38

wainscoting on the wall. Then she cleared her throat. "Do you always take pictures of strange girls in hotel lobbies?" she said in a proper upper-class British accent.

"What?" Joe said, spinning around with an innocent expression.

Frank bent toward Nancy as if to point something out to her. His face was crimson with suppressed laughter. "The Don Juan of Bayport!" he whispered. "Caught red-handed!"

The girl wasn't buying Joe's "innocent" act. She folded her arms and said, "The least you can do is send me a copy."

"Right," Joe answered with an embarrassed laugh. "I'm sorry. I was taking some *architectural* shots, and I guess I got a little carried away. You're very photogenic, you know."

The girl's face broke into a warm grin. "Oh? Are you a professional?"

"Well, no, not really," Joe answered. "Just an amateur with an eye for beauty."

"Oh, please," Frank said almost inaudibly.

But to Nancy it looked as if Joe might get what he wanted.

The girl held out a long, graceful arm to Joe. "I'm Fiona Fox," she said sweetly.

Frank shook his head in disbelief. "Incredible," he murmured.

"Joe Hardy," Joe said cheerfully. He took her hand and squeezed it gently.

"Lovely to meet you, Joe," Fiona replied.

"Oh! The pleasure is mine, I'm sure."

"'The pleasure is mine, I'm sure,'" Frank repeated, rolling his eyes.

"Sshhh!" Nancy hissed. She was enjoying eavesdropping on Joe.

But Joe had begun glancing at his watch, looking guilty and uncomfortable. "Well, I'm supposed to be meeting my brother right now. See you soon, Fiona!"

"I hope so," Fiona answered with another dazzling smile tossed over her shoulder as she headed back up to her table.

With a slightly shame-faced grin, Joe turned toward Frank and Nancy. Frank shook his head in mock reproof. "Hate to butt in on your social life, Romeo," he said, "but I hear we're supposed to be working on a case."

"Hey, listen, I've already taken two rolls of suspects!" Joe exclaimed. "There just wasn't anybody suspicious around at that moment! So I was searching for angles, and—"

"Well, it looks as though you found curves," Frank interrupted. "Come on, let's go see what you've got. Nancy and I are at a dead end."

Frank and Joe had transformed their bathroom into a mini-darkroom. With Nancy's help, they developed Joe's film and then painstakingly made black-and-white prints.

As the three of them were poring over the pictures with a magnifying glass afterward, there was a knock at the door.

"I'm back from Paradise!" Bess's voice called from the hall.

Joe opened the door, and Bess practically floated in. "We just saw the most *wonderful* show! You wouldn't believe the dancing—and one of the songs made me cry! John bought me a cast album—"

And she proceeded to give them a rapturous dance-by-dance, song-by-song description. Nancy, Frank, and Joe all listened patiently, and Nancy knew they were sharing a common thought. Bess was becoming part of the problem instead of the solution.

Tip-tip-tip-tip.

Nancy's eyes flicked open. She looked over and saw Bess in her bed. Where was that noise coming from?

Tip-tip-tip-tip. The window!

With catlike stealth, Nancy stepped out of bed and peered behind the drapes.

"I thought you'd never hear me!" came a soft voice.

Nancy took a deep breath, her heart thudding in her chest. "You know, John," she said angrily, "there's nothing wrong with using the hallway."

"Please, just let me in," John pleaded. "I don't have much time!"

He sounded desperate. Nancy quickly opened the window, and John climbed in. "You've got to help me get out of here!" he said urgently.

Suddenly Bess stirred and sat bolt upright in her bed. "*John!*" she gasped.

"Yes, it's me," John said. "I'm afraid I can't say much. But there are some people after me. I tried to climb out my window to the street, but someone is stationed on the sidewalk just below my room. I need a disguise."

"Sure, John!" Bess said. "I'll find something—" She grabbed her robe from the end of the bed and threw it on.

"Hold on a second," Nancy said firmly. She reached for her robe as she flicked on a light. "We're not doing anything until we talk to Frank and Joe."

"Yes. Of course—but hurry!" John said.

Nancy punched Frank and Joe's number on the phone and told a groggy Frank the story.

"But he may be the guy we're looking for!" Frank said.

"Exactly!" Nancy answered tersely. She didn't want to say anything more within earshot of John.

"I know—you can't talk," said Frank. "But I can tell what you're thinking. If we help him leave the hotel, we may find out what he's up to. We'll be right there!"

At first glance no one would have paid any attention to the group of five teenagers leaving the building. Frank, Joe, Nancy, and Bess appeared to be about as normal as could be—and so did the tall guy between Nancy and Bess.

At least he looked normal from a distance. Up close it was easy to tell that his mustache and beard stubble were painted on with gray eye shadow, that his trench coat was too small, and his wool knit winter hat was pulled down a little too far over his eyes.

"Just don't talk to anyone," Nancy whispered to John as they pushed through the revolving lobby door.

"Uh-huh," John mumbled.

Nancy breathed a sigh of relief as they stepped out onto the sidewalk. Safe so far!

"All right. Let's get a cab," Frank said.

Suddenly a black-gloved hand landed on Frank's shoulder. "Not so fast," a gravelly voice snarled.

Frank swung around to face a broad-shouldered, pug-faced man. "Hey, what do you think you're doing?" he demanded.

"Putting you under arrest," the man said. He opened a small leather case in his hand and revealed a police badge. "Sergeant Kolody, New York City Police."

"We're under arrest?" Joe laughed. "Why? Is there a curfew in New York City?"

"No, there isn't," the man retorted. He narrowed his eyes and glared at Joe. "But there *is* a law against kidnapping Crown Prince Jean-Claude of Sarconne!"

Chapter
Five

"Wʜᴀᴛ?"

The cry rose in unison from Frank, Joe, Nancy, and Bess.

"Very good," Sergeant Kolody growled. "A couple more rehearsals and you'll make a barbershop quartet."

John ripped off his wool hat and sighed. "I had a feeling this would happen," he said.

"You mean it's true?" Bess said, swaying backward.

"I'm afraid so." John—or Jean-Claude—shrugged. "I *do* have an explanation, though."

"I can't wait to hear this one," Joe said.

"All right, you hoodlums," Sergeant Kolody

said, grabbing Frank and Joe by the shoulders. "*You're* the ones who're going to be doing the explaining—in court!"

"No!" Jean-Claude commanded, in a loud, firm voice that startled everyone. They all froze and stared at him.

"Sorry," Jean-Claude said. "That's a bad habit I picked up from my father. We call it the Royal No."

"Excuse me, Your Excellency?" Sergeant Kolody said.

"Highness was okay," Jean-Claude said. "Anyway, you can let go of them, Sergeant. I won't tell your supervisors anything."

Sergeant Kolody looked baffled. "My supervisors? I don't understand."

"It's just that I wouldn't want you to get in trouble for impeding the progress of a visiting dignitary. I'm sure you don't *mean* to create an international incident."

"International—"

"No need to apologize," Jean-Claude said magnanimously. "I guess it's easy to forget that visiting dignitaries sometimes have to travel incognito to avoid publicity."

Sergeant Kolody's face was beet red now. He wiped beads of sweat off his brow. Nancy and Frank exchanged a knowing look. They could see that Jean-Claude had completely unraveled him.

At that moment a slim, balding man with a pencil-thin mustache stepped through the revolving door of the Winslow. Looking impatiently left and right, he pulled the fur collar of his cashmere coat tightly around his neck. Finally his eyes lit on Jean-Claude, and he did a double take.

"There you are!" the man said. His eyebrows drew together into a frown as he approached. "Officer, *I* shall take custody of the young man. Thank you for your good work."

Sergeant Kolody quickly started backing away. "Sure thing, Count Reynaud," he said meekly. "He's all yours." With that, the police officer disappeared around the corner.

Jean-Claude turned to Nancy and her friends before they could say a word. With an embarrassed smile, he said, "I apologize that you learned my secret this way. I wasn't attempting to deceive you. I just needed another identity." He glanced over at Count Reynaud and then back at Bess. "Someday I'll explain it all to you. I promise."

Bess just stared at him. "I—I still can't believe it," she said after a moment.

"Neither can I," said Frank. "How did you—"

"Please, Your Highness," Count Reynaud cut in. "I need some sleep. I have been up all night trying to determine your whereabouts. You may chat with your friends, if that is what they are, another time."

Jean-Claude shrugged. "I'm sorry, cousin. I didn't realize you were upset."

"Didn't realize I was upset?" Count Reynaud's

eyes burned with rage. "I turned around this morning after your photo session and you were gone! You had evaded all your bodyguards. Fortunately, the luncheon afterward was a formality, so I could cover for you. But to miss the meeting at the American consulate? Our country's highest-ranking representative just decided not to attend? I had no idea if you had been abducted or not."

Jean-Claude's face turned red. "You're right, of course, cousin."

"Of course I am!" Reynaud snapped. "And frankly, I don't wish to discuss this in public. For the sake of our country, my sanity, and your well-being, I suggest we return to our suite—now."

Reynaud stood aside to allow Jean-Claude to precede him to the front door. "After you, Your Highness." He chose to ignore Nancy and her friends completely.

But Jean-Claude didn't. Instead of moving toward the revolving door, he turned to them. "This gentleman is Count Reynaud—my father's cousin by marriage. He and my father do not see eye to eye politically—and as a punishment, my cousin is given charge of me whenever we travel alone." Stopping just before the door, he threw them a quick wink. "I can't quite figure it out, but I always want to get *away* from him," he whispered loud enough for Reynaud to hear.

"Good night," Count Reynaud said stiffly, a

slight nod in their direction. "I hope to have the pleasure of making all of your acquaintances at another time."

As the two men disappeared into the hotel, Nancy watched as Jean-Claude put his arm around Reynaud's shoulder. "So what'll it be, cousin?" he asked casually. "An exciting game of canasta?" Then as the men moved into the lobby she could hear no more.

Nancy watched Frank. His expression mirrored exactly what she was feeling—a little amusement, a little anger, a little shock.

And a *lot* of confusion.

"I—I still can't believe it!" said Bess the next afternoon. "Prince Jean-Claude of Sarconne. I couldn't sleep all night thinking about him. And now we're all going to have lunch with him!"

Nancy laughed as she unfolded the linen napkin and placed it in her lap. "Yes, it is pretty incredible. He went from being a cat burglar to a prince in five minutes—like a character from a fairy tale."

Nancy, Bess, Frank, and Joe were waiting for the prince in the Winslow's main dining area, an oak-paneled room, lavishly decorated for Christmas. Huge juniper wreaths swagged with gold ribbons hung on all the walls, and on each table was an arrangement of holly and other greens in a low crystal vase flanked by gold candles protected by glass hurricane jars.

"So where is the prince?" Joe asked. "I'm starving!"

"Please go ahead and order," came Jean-Claude's voice just then. They watched as Jean-Claude and Count Reynaud walked up to their table.

"How do you do, Your Highness?" Bess said, jumping to her feet and curtsying.

Nancy winced, and a look of utter disgust crossed Joe's face.

But Jean-Claude only laughed. "Never call me that again! It's Jean-Claude to you." With a twinkle in his eye, he added in a stage whisper, "But you had better call *him* Count Reynaud, or he'll be upset."

"*Really,* Jean-Claude!" Count Reynaud said indignantly, joining the others at the table.

Jean-Claude smiled broadly at Reynaud. "I am only teasing you, cousin. These are my friends whom you so briefly met last night—Bess Marvin, Nancy Drew, and Frank and Joe Hardy."

Reynaud greeted each with a tight little smile and a curt nod.

Frank, who had stood, reached across the table to shake the count's hand.

Count Reynaud looked at Frank's hand as if it were a live snake. He did briefly shake it, though, before sitting down. "Prince Jean-Claude has asked me to extend to all of you an invitation to a preview party this afternoon to view the crown jewels before the exhibit is open to the general public at the Metropolitan Museum."

"Great!" Bess said.

"Having you accompany him will make the party more tolerable for Jean-Claude," Reynaud continued.

Jean-Claude chuckled. "Thanks, cousin. That is very thoughtful of you."

Reynaud didn't answer, but only gave the prince a hard stare.

"Yes, I know," Jean-Claude said in answer to the stare. "I'll hold up my end of the bargain." He turned to the others. "I promised Cousin Reynaud I'd apologize to you for last night. I didn't mean to cause you so much trouble."

"Trouble? It was fun!" Bess said.

"Yes, it was," Nancy agreed. "Have you always been a rebel?"

"Yes," Jean-Claude said wistfully. "I think I wasn't born to be a prince. You have no idea what it's like living from ceremony to ceremony, surrounded by stuffy, boring people, always overdressed in stiff, formal clothes." He glanced over to Reynaud. "Present company excluded, of course!" he said ironically.

Reynaud cleared his throat and looked off into the distance.

"My parents let me take up mountaineering because they thought it would eliminate my restlessness and boredom." He shrugged. "But as you've seen, it only made it worse. Now I can't even be in the same place for more than a few minutes without feeling the need to escape!"

"So *that's* why you sneaked through our window," Bess said. She gasped and put her hand to her mouth. "Or shouldn't I have said that?"

Jean-Claude chuckled. "Oh, my cousin knows now. He always suspected I'd climb out the window. In fact, he stationed a bodyguard on the sidewalk below our third-floor suite. But he didn't realize I might climb *upward* to escape!"

"Yes, well . . ." Count Reynaud said, raising his eyebrows. "I trust we've come to a slightly more liberal agreement. Now, we shall be leaving directly after lunch. Will all four of you be accompanying us?"

"We travel together," Nancy said.

"Indeed," Count Reynaud said with a sniff. "So be it." And he subsided into a chilly silence for the rest of the meal.

Lunch was lively for everyone else and thrilling for Bess. Whenever Jean-Claude's eyes and hers met, everyone else vanished for them, and they were alone.

After lunch they picked up their coats and met in the lobby. Jean-Claude and Bess, arm in arm, led the little band out into the clean, cold afternoon sunshine.

While they waited for Jean-Claude's limo, Bess leaned close to the prince, talking and laughing with him.

Frank spoke to Joe and Nancy. "I have a

feeling that from here on in, there are only *three* of us on this case."

Nancy sighed. It looked as though Bess really was lost to them now. Bess with a crown prince, she thought. They'd never stop hearing about it in River Heights.

Joe eyed Bess and Jean-Claude as they disappeared into the stretch limo. Before climbing in himself, he whispered to Frank and Nancy. "I *still* don't trust him, prince or no prince."

Nancy thought over the past couple of days' events and had to admit Joe had a point.

Frank felt out of place in the special exhibit room at the Metropolitan Museum. Everyone there was either foreign or three times his age. Also, his corduroy jacket, white oxford-cloth shirt, chinos, and deck shoes stuck out among the custom-tailored suits all the other men were wearing. He hadn't packed anything for an occasion such as this.

He and Joe circled the room, stopping briefly in front of a large glass case. Inside the case was a heavy solid-gold crown studded with sapphires, rubies, and emeralds.

"I'll bet it took a lot of proof-of-purchase seals to get this baby," Joe said.

Frank leaned back against the guardrail surrounding the case. "They say it's one of the most spectacular crowns in the world."

"Seems strange to leave it out in the open like

this when they're so worried it's going to be stolen."

Frank shook his head. "Well, judging from their other crimes, the burglars are probably laying low right now. They only come out for big, spectacular scenes."

"Like when the jewels are over at the U.N. gala."

"Exactly. This group is too small, too controlled. Besides, Jean-Claude tells me half the people here are undercover guards."

"We'll be closing in twenty minutes," a uniformed museum guard said to Frank and Joe. Just then Frank noticed Jean-Claude and Bess heading their way. Jean-Claude had a devilish smile on his face, and Bess was looking over her shoulder.

"Quick," Jean-Claude said to the brothers. "Reynaud is in a deep conversation with my bodyguard about his family history. They'll be engrossed till they shut off the lights. I'll tell them I'm going into the men's room and slip out and meet you in front of the museum. We'll have just enough time for a trip into Central Park."

"Wait a minute!" Joe said.

But Jean-Claude swept past them and over to his cousin and guard. Nancy and Bess were close behind. "Come on," Bess said to Frank and Joe.

Frank checked over his shoulder. Reynaud *was* deep in conversation with the guard. He nodded to Joe, and they left.

Minutes later the five of them were trotting down the front steps of the Met and into the dark twilight. Jean-Claude and Bess, holding hands, took the steps two at a time.

Nancy saw Jean-Claude's limo parked against the curb under a streetlight. It was squeezed between an economy car and a dark gray van. A street vendor just in front of the van was calling out, "Chestnuts! Hot! Here's your chestnuts!"

"Ooooh," Bess said. "Those smell good—and warm!"

Jean-Claude stopped short. "Your every wish is my command!" he said, reaching into his pocket. He walked away from the others to the vendor and said, "Five bags of your biggest, hottest chestnuts. Keep the change." He held out a twenty-dollar bill.

"Sure, buddy," the vendor said. He pocketed the money. As Jean-Claude reached out for the first bag, the vendor grabbed his wrist and wrenched it sideways so that Jean-Claude stumbled and lost his balance.

"Wha-what's going on?" Jean-Claude said.

"Just want to make sure I gave you the right bag." With a strong yank, he pulled Jean-Claude around to the back of the cart.

Unable to turn around and face his attacker, Jean-Claude kicked behind him, smashing his heel into the vendor's kneecap. The man cursed, but didn't loosen his hold. He'd had the advantage of surprise, and he'd managed to get Jean-

54

Claude so firmly that the prince couldn't free himself.

Frank looked over, saw what was happening, and ran toward the cart. Joe and Nancy followed close behind.

At the same time a man in a black mask jumped out of the back of the van. "Stay back!" he shouted—and pointed a revolver straight at Frank.

Frank froze. The two men dragged Jean-Claude, kicking and struggling, toward the van. "Take your hands off me!" Jean-Claude shouted. "I'll get the entire U.N. after you!"

"Save it." With a vicious shove the masked man pushed Jean-Claude into the back. The vendor raced around to the driver's seat.

"Help him!" Bess screamed. "Somebody help him!"

But there was nothing anyone could do—not while the masked man was pointing the gun right at them. He climbed in and slammed the door, his gun still leveled at Frank.

With an ugly shriek of its tires, the van sped away.

"Jean-Claude!" Bess cried out, her face white in the artificial glow from the streetlight.

All four of them stood openmouthed as the van disappeared. They caught a glimpse of Jean-Claude banging desperately on the rear window, his face twisted with the realization that he was helpless.

Chapter

Six

QUICK! THE LIMO!" Nancy cried out. She, Frank, Joe, and Bess all raced to Jean-Claude's limousine. Nancy glanced down Fifth Avenue, hoping to see the van tied up in traffic. But as she looked, the van swerved to the right, leaped onto the curb, and plowed down the sidewalk, scattering pedestrians to either side of it.

The limo driver was sound asleep, his head lolling back against the seat. Joe pushed him aside and hopped in, grabbing the steering wheel.

"Huh? Hey, what's going on?" the driver mumbled. Straightening up, he struggled to push Joe out of the car as Nancy, Bess, and Frank slid into the backseat.

Suddenly the passenger door swung open, and a hand grabbed at the driver's shoulder. "Let go of him, François!" Count Reynaud cried out, and he climbed into the front seat.

"I saw what happened." He turned to Joe. "Perhaps *now* you see why the prince requires a chaperon and bodyguard!" he said icily.

Joe gunned the accelerator, and the limo screeched off.

"I saw them go right at that light!" Nancy said, pointing. As Joe turned the limo sharply, Nancy was jerked to the left and sent sprawling across the seat into Frank's lap.

"Sorry," she said, quickly sitting up. On either side of the car, barren trees whizzed by, lit up by the old-fashioned black iron streetlights. They must be in Central Park, Nancy realized. She grabbed onto the door handrest as the limo veered first left, then right.

"Watch out for those joggers!" Bess screamed. Directly ahead of them, a group of four people, with Day-Glo tape on their running suits, was trotting slowly down a hill. Hearing a car approach rapidly, they looked back over their shoulders. Panic shot into their eyes. One of them ducked to the right, one to the left, and the other two froze, caught in the beams from the headlights.

H-O-O-O-NK! Nancy lurched forward as Joe blasted the horn and slammed on the brake. At the last moment, the two joggers in the center dove for the side of the road.

As Joe plowed past, they could see the foursome mouthing complaints. But they heard nothing with the windows rolled up. Joe wiped at his forehead with his left hand and steered with the right as he wove in and out of traffic for the next couple of minutes.

"There's the van! Up ahead!" Nancy cried. The taillights of the van, like two glowing eyes, sped out of sight around a sharp bend just ahead.

"Hang on!" Joe said through gritted teeth, blasting the horn. The limo practically lifted off the ground as it hugged the curves and avoided the other cars.

"Please! This car is not meant to be driven like this!" the chauffeur yelled, trying to grab the steering wheel.

"Stop that at once, François!" Count Reynaud commanded, yanking the man's hands away from Joe. As Reynaud looked forward again, Nancy noticed that the corners of his lips turned up into a tiny smile. For the first time since they'd met him, the count actually looked as if he were enjoying himself. Why? Nancy wondered.

The two cars twisted snakelike around the other cars. First around the north side of Central Park and then down the west side. They passed a small frozen lake and some tennis courts.

"We're gaining on them!" Bess yelled over the blare of the horn.

Joe began pulling the limo to the left as both cars ran a red light. They were the only two vehicles on the road now. Nancy knew he was going to try to drive beside the van and force it over.

"Come on, you two-ton bucket of bolts," Joe said as the front of the limo began to pass the rear of the van. Nancy held her breath. In seconds they would be beside the van. She craned her neck to see if she could spot Jean-Claude through the side window, but the interior was much too dark.

SCREEEEEEK! With a bone-jarring jolt, Nancy, Bess, and Frank found themselves hurtling against the front seat. Nancy's eyes darted up, for through the windshield she could see two riders leading their horses across the road toward the bridle path on the other side.

The riders dropped the reins and jumped onto the side of the road.

"The horses! Move the horses!" Joe shouted frantically as if the riders could hear him. But the big, lumbering animals just stood there, paralyzed by the headlights and noise.

Nancy felt her stomach jump up into her throat. The limo fishtailed along the road, passing the van with its tires squealing. The horses were only a few feet away now.

Bess let out an ear-splitting shriek.

And suddenly, the car slammed to a dead standstill as if it had hit something.

"Di-did we kill them?" Bess asked in a tiny voice. She had been thrown to the floor, and was cowering there now, her hands over her eyes.

Nancy looked up. Directly in front of the car

was the broad, dark brown flank of a quarter horse.

The horse threw back its head and whinnied, then trotted calmly off to its rider, alive and untouched.

"Way to go, Joe," Frank said softly.

"You—you did it!" Bess gasped.

"Oh, my heart!" said Count Reynaud, clutching his chest.

"My *car!*" moaned François.

Frank rolled down the window. The van had left the road fifteen feet farther back and was now resting atop a knoll. He didn't see Jean-Claude or his kidnappers.

"Where do you think you are—the Indy Five Hundred?" cried one of the riders from outside the car. "Hey—*hey!* What are you doing with those horses?"

Frank didn't realize he'd opened his door until he was out on the road, Nancy, Joe, and Bess right behind him.

The chestnut vendor had run up and scrambled onto one of the horses, and the masked man was now trying to force Jean-Claude up onto the other horse.

Nancy, Frank, Joe, and Bess rushed Jean-Claude. The kidnappers suddenly looked up— and instantly the masked man drew his revolver. He fired a single warning shot over their heads.

"Get down!" Frank shouted.

The four of them hit the hard-packed earth as

the riderless horse reared off the ground, yanking the reins from the hands of the masked kidnapper.

Cursing, the masked man struggled with his horse. And in the confusion Jean-Claude broke away from the kidnappers.

"Forget it!" the vendor shouted. "Let's get out of here!"

The masked kidnapper clumsily mounted the horse. Then, with a swift kick, he set the horse in motion, and the two men galloped off beside the oncoming traffic.

Nancy and Bess went straight for Jean-Claude, and Frank and Joe dashed off in pursuit of the kidnappers.

"You poor thing!" Bess said, stroking Jean-Claude's hair. "Are you all right?"

"Is *he* all right?" a voice barked before Jean-Claude could answer. "What about *us?*" Nancy and Bess looked up to see the two riders, their faces lit up by the slowly moving cars, glowering down at them. One of them was hysterically pointing a finger in the direction the kidnappers had gone. "Do you know how much it cost to rent those horses?" she shrieked. "I hope your friends intend to reimburse us!"

Nancy and Bess silently looked at each other, and then back at the riders. They'd managed to rescue Jean-Claude, but it was clear that their problems were far from over.

* * *

"Oh-h-h, o-h-h. Party till you drop . . ."

Music blared through the loudspeaker as a waitress slapped down a basket of tortilla chips and a bowl of guacamole on the table.

Count Reynaud shook his head. "'Party till you drop'?" he repeated in disgust.

Jean-Claude let out a hearty laugh. "Loosen up, cousin. This is a celebration! You didn't lose me to kidnappers after all!"

The prince had insisted on bringing Nancy, Frank, Bess, and Joe to his favorite Mexican restaurant, a huge cavernlike place on the Upper East Side, after they'd made sure he was all right. Count Reynaud and the prince's bodyguards had come along, too.

Bess beamed at Jean-Claude now. "I can't believe how calm you are."

"Really," Nancy said. "You recovered so quickly. And you did a great job of calming down those riders."

Jean-Claude chuckled. "Well, it was the least I could do. Frank and Joe had the difficult job. Bringing back the horses."

Frank nodded. "I only wish we'd gotten those guys, but they took off through the woods on foot. The van was totally unmarked—no license, nothing. Of absolutely no use."

"Well, you did a great job rescuing me," Jean-Claude said. "Which brings me to the question I want to ask you." He placed his forearms on the table and gazed at Frank and Joe and Nancy. His face had grown serious. "It's obvious you are true professionals with brains and cunning. It's also obvious that I'm in danger and need more protection than my bodyguards can offer." He glanced at Count Reynaud, who had raised his eyebrows practically to his hairline. "Now—I propose that you act as my personal bodyguards while I'm in New York."

"Never!" Count Reynaud exclaimed.

Joe raised one of his hands, palm out. "Hate to burst your bubble, Prince, but we're on a case of our own."

"A case?" Jean-Claude asked.

Joe and Frank exchanged a look. A tense silence hung in the air. Frank paused for a moment, then let out a deep breath. "All right, we'll tell you," he said. "You're not the only one who was keeping a secret. Frank, Nancy, and I are private detectives. We're in New York on a case. Bess is helping us."

Jean-Claude's eyes lit up. "Detectives," he repeated slowly. "That makes sense. You must be after the two thieves whom everyone in the Sarconne embassy is afraid of. What do they call them? Cat burglars?"

"Right," Joe said.

Jean-Claude appeared to be thinking something over. Then a slow smile spread across his face. He shook his head and let out a low chuckle. "This is wonderful."

"What is?" Nancy asked.

"Well, my offer just may help you as much as it will help me." Jean-Claude's expression became deadly serious again as he looked from Nancy to Frank to Joe. "I believe I can prove that my would-be kidnappers are none other than your cat burglars."

Chapter

Seven

WHAT!" THE SINGLE WORD came out of everyone's mouth in a chorus. Jean-Claude sat back, obviously enjoying the attention.

"I may not be a detective," he said, "but I do know that Sarconne intelligence has some information about the burglars. There are two suspects, one of them older than the other—and that description *exactly* fits my kidnappers."

Joe looked at him blankly. "That's it? The whole ball of wax? I mean, that's what *we* know already."

"Well, it confirms our source's information," Nancy interjected. "But why would burglars kidnap Jean-Claude? That's not their line of work."

"True," they all said. Jean-Claude thought about it for a moment. "Maybe it hadn't been planned. They could have been lurking outside the Met, casing the place. Then they saw *me* come out, without my cousin or bodyguards, and . . ."

Frank nodded. "I guess they could have done it on the spur of the moment."

"Kidnapping can be very lucrative, you know," Jean-Claude said.

Nancy could see that Frank and Joe were mulling it over. "I think we should check it out, guys," she suggested. "We don't have too many leads."

"But how?" Frank said, more to himself than the others.

After a second Joe nodded his head, but Nancy could tell from his expression that he wasn't entirely convinced.

"Good!" Jean-Claude said. In a mock-regal voice, he intoned, "Then with the power vested in me by the monarchy of Sarconne, I hereby dub thee royal bodyguards—"

"I *beg* your pardon," Count Reynaud broke in. "But I believe I have a say in this matter. I would like to talk to you privately, Jean-Claude." He rose from the table and motioned for Jean-Claude's bodyguards to remain where they were, at each of the doors. "Excuse us, please," he said to Nancy and her friends.

Reynaud turned and walked stiffly across the restaurant, his shoulders pulled back square and his chin up. Jean-Claude shrugged. "I'd better see what he wants," he said.

Nancy watched as Jean-Claude trailed Reynaud across the restaurant and then disappeared behind an enormous Christmas tree, which blocked the front entrance from Nancy's table.

"Are they going outside?" Bess said. "They'll freeze!"

Nancy craned her neck, but she couldn't see. Quite abruptly she stood up. "I'll be right back," she said decisively.

"Where are you going?" Joe asked.

"I want to hear what they're saying," Nancy replied quietly.

Bess looked a little shocked. "Don't you think that's kind of—"

"Improper?" Nancy finished for her. "No, just professional. If we're part of this case, we need to know what's going on. And I don't trust the count to tell us."

Nancy snaked her way between the tables toward the front entrance. Just before the Christmas tree, she stopped at the coat rack, unhooked Count Reynaud's coat and Jean-Claude's jacket, and folded them over her arm. If anyone asked, she could pretend that she'd followed them to bring them their coats. She had just started to walk around the tree when the sound of voices stopped her.

"This can only *please* my parents. They'll be perfect bodyguards!"

It was Jean-Claude. Nancy froze. He and Rey-

A Nancy Drew & Hardy Boys SuperMystery

naud *hadn't* gone outside. They had stopped in a small area between the tree and the front vestibule.

Nancy backed away and held up a finger to Frank. She gestured with her chin to show him where Jean-Claude and his cousin were. Then she crept closer into the sheltering branches of the tree, hoping no one would pay any attention to her.

Jean-Claude was still speaking. "Besides," he continued, "I won't feel the need to escape from you."

"You may joke all you like. But, Jean-Claude, you have to understand how humiliating it is for me to have you reach outside the accepted sources of our security. Besides, these acquaintances of yours are—are—"

"Are *what,* Cousin Reynaud?" Jean-Claude said flatly, as if he knew exactly what Reynaud was about to say.

"All right, I'll say it. They're *common!* Common, overeager Americans with their own interests at heart! Don't you see I have *your* interests at heart? And need I spell out the motives of people like that—that *fortune huntress*—what's her name, Beth Melvin?"

Nancy recoiled inwardly. How dare he accuse Bess of pursuing Jean-Claude for his money!

When Jean-Claude spoke, his voice was taut with anger. "It's *Bess,* Cousin Reynaud. Bess Marvin. And for your information, those 'common' Americans happen to be the only people

68

I've met here worth spending time with. They're the only people who look at me for who I am—who see me as a person, not a title! Obviously that doesn't mean much to you."

Nancy knew Count Reynaud was smoldering as he answered, "As you wish, then. I shall say no more about it."

Nancy turned and threw the coats back onto the hooks and rushed to her chair.

"What did they say?" Bess asked as Nancy sat down.

"Never mind!" Nancy said. "They're coming! And I don't see *how* anyone could wear a skirt that length!" she said brightly to Bess, as if they'd been discussing fashion the whole time Jean-Claude and his cousin were away.

When they returned to the table, Reynaud stood behind his chair and said, in a voice as icy as the air outside, "The prince and I have agreed you shall be his bodyguards, effective immediately."

Bess clapped her hands. "I think this calls for a celebration! How about a round of desserts?"

"Why not?" Reynaud said. "You're not paying for it."

His comment hung in the air as if a gray cloud had moved in.

"Or—or maybe not," Bess quickly added, looking embarrassed. "They're a little expensive, I think."

Jean-Claude laughed. "Please, don't be silly."

"Yes, there'll be plenty of money left over for

the diamonds and furs," Reynaud murmured, just loud enough for everyone to hear.

The silence at the table was broken only by an occasional request and a few nervous, unhappy sighs from Bess.

Nancy slammed down the phone. "I don't know how he does it—but *now's* not the time!" She sprang up from the desk in her room.

"What was that all about?" Frank asked, looking up from the notes they had been studying.

"That was Jean-Claude. He wanted to know where Bess was. I told him she's on surveillance duty in the lobby. He said, 'Fine. I'll pick her up there'!" She went to the door and yanked it open. "We'd better go and stop him."

Frank followed her out to the elevator. "Well, he won't get past Joe. Don't forget, we stationed him in Jean-Claude's hallway."

"I wouldn't be too sure. He did get past Reynaud and three or four bodyguards."

When they arrived in the lobby, Nancy noticed Joe. She was about to call him when a voice from the balcony—a girl's voice, with a British accent—stopped her short.

"Where's your camera?"

Joe looked up. "Oh, hi!" he answered enthusiastically.

Leaning over the balcony wrapped with pine garlands and golden ribbons was Fiona Fox, the girl Joe had photographed. Next to her was a distinguished-looking gray-haired man in tweeds. "You want to join Dad and me for hot chocolate?" Fiona asked Joe.

Joe spotted Frank and Nancy, mouthed, "Just for a minute," at them, and hurried to the stairs.

"I'll talk to him about this later," Frank said. "Let's find—"

Just then Count Reynaud rushed out of the elevator and up to them. "Where is he?" he demanded furiously.

"We were about to ask you that," Nancy said. "Didn't you see him leave? It would just have been a few minutes ago."

"When I just went in to check on him, I found clothes stuffed under his sheet. He has sneaked out again—past all of you."

"Excuse me a second," Nancy interrupted. Joe was signaling to her from the bottom of the stairs. She walked over to him, leaving Frank and the count alone.

"We thought we'd lost you," she said to Joe.

"You mean to the Foxes? I just told them I'd see them later," Joe said. "I wouldn't walk off." He pointed to a sofa in a secluded niche of the lobby. "Look over there—you'll see why."

With Nancy following, Joe waltzed over to the sofa, hands on hips, and asked, "Private enough back here?"

Jean-Claude and Bess looked up sheepishly from the corner of the sofa where they'd been cuddling. "Joe, it's not what it looks like," Bess said hastily. "Jean-Claude wanted to help me figure out who the cat burglars could be."

71

"I was getting cabin fever in my room, you see—" Jean-Claude added.

"So you climbed out the window and called my room from a pay phone," Nancy said, finishing his sentence.

Jean-Claude smiled. "You *are* a detective!" He stood with Bess beside him.

"And *you* figured the most logical place for suspects would be behind a couch," Joe said wryly.

"Well, actually," Bess said, "when we saw Count Reynaud storm off the elevator, we ducked behind the couch."

Just then Reynaud's voice echoed through the lobby. "*There* you are!" He marched toward Jean-Claude, his shoulders hunched. Frank followed closely behind.

"Hello, Cousin Reynaud," Jean-Claude said calmly.

"'Hello, Cousin Reynaud,'" the count mimicked acidly. "I believe I am owed an explanation, Jean-Claude. You've alienated not only me, but also your friend Frank and his girlfriend."

Girlfriend? Nancy was taken aback for a moment. But she knew that now wasn't the time to correct Reynaud.

"You will have the explanation you want," Jean-Claude said. "I realized that Bess was—"

Reynaud threw out his hand, cutting him off. "I'd prefer to talk upstairs in private."

Jean-Claude laughed. "Oh, please, Reynaud. I

only wanted to speak with Bess. Must we retire to the tomb—"

"Young man," Reynaud said through tightly clenched teeth. "You may think of me as old and stuffy, but there are some things that experience teaches—like the value of privacy! And as you can guess, I'm not only talking about *our* conflict." His face was becoming redder and redder. "I'm talking about your public display of affection with this—this—" He stared at Bess, his face twisted into an expression of sheer disgust. "This lower-class golddigger!"

Bess shrank back in shock, and Jean-Claude's mouth dropped open. His voice vibrated with fury when he finally did speak.

"I don't believe you said that, Cousin Reynaud. It certainly wasn't a very *private* way to express your opinion, was it?" He jumped to his feet and took a step toward Reynaud, his eyes dark with rage. "In fact, not only was it public, it was rude—to Bess *and* to me! I demand a written apology—*with* a copy to my parents."

At first Nancy thought Reynaud would roar in anger at Jean-Claude. But instead he just stared at the prince, his face softening more and more. Finally he looked indecisive and took a step backward. "I—I do apologize, Jean-Claude. To you and Miss Marvin. Of course I didn't mean what I said." He looked so contrite that Nancy almost felt sorry for him. "Let me make it up to you."

"Well . . ." Jean-Claude said. "By now you should know there is only one thing that would make both Bess and me happy."

"Yes?" Reynaud asked.

"A night on the town—without you!"

"W-E-E-E-E-E-A-A-A-A-A-A-A-A-H-H-H!" The lead guitarist did a split in the air. After landing he fell onto his back, writhing and kicking. But this neither interrupted his playing nor caused his spiky hair to move an inch.

As Nancy and Frank sipped their soft drinks, they watched Joe dance with a raven-haired girl he'd just met. Above him, three girls in black leather outfits were singing backup vocals from a huge steel cage. Beside the far wall, Jean-Claude and Bess were gazing into each other's eyes and smiling as they swayed to the beat, not even bothering to dance. Four black doors behind Jean-Claude and Bess were labeled Tunnels 1, 2, 3, and 4, and a large, hand-painted sign above the doors said "Underground: Maximum age 19" in jagged black letters.

"I wonder where those tunnels go," Nancy mused.

"A couple to storage rooms," Frank said. "The others lead to the sidewalk. The doors used to be hidden."

Nancy gave him a skeptical look. "How do you know all this?"

"I read about this place in a guidebook," Frank said. "During Prohibition, there was a speakeasy

74

down here. The shop owner on the first floor used to let people in through a trapdoor. Illegal booze was concealed in the hidden storage rooms, and if the place was raided, people escaped through the tunnels. Now the tunnels are just fancy fire exits."

"I'm impressed," Nancy said.

When Frank smiled at her, the subdued lighting softened the sharp angles of his handsome face.

"You should be," he replied. "Now that you're my 'girlfriend,' I have to do things to impress you."

Nancy looked at him blankly. It *sounded* as if he was joking, but why would he say something like—

Frank caught her confused glance. "Reynaud's comment—in the lobby," he said, reminding her. "Remember? He referred to you as my girlfriend." He laughed and shook his head.

"Oh. Right," Nancy said softly. Suddenly her throat felt as if it were coated with cotton. "Imagine that, you and me . . ." She meant to laugh it off, but the remark came out sounding wistful.

Great, Nancy, she thought. Make a total fool of both of us. Make him feel obligated to talk about his girlfriend, Callie Shaw—which will make *you* obligated to talk about Ned!

But Frank looked back at her with a warm smile. He didn't appear to be embarrassed. "Yeah, imagine," he said gently, his brown eyes shining. He gazed at Nancy for minutes, as if trying to come up with the perfect way to phrase something. Nancy couldn't help but look away. She thought he might see her blush.

"Nancy?" Frank said quietly and urgently.

"Yes? What, Frank?"

He started up from his chair. "Four guys in ski masks just came in."

Nancy turned toward him, puzzled. "Well, it is supposed to get really cold tonight."

"Uh-uh," Frank continued, his voice tense. "These guys just came in through one of the tunnels behind Bess and Jean-Claude!"

Nancy whirled around. Two of the men were standing against the wall by the exit door. The other two were walking around. They seemed to be doing nothing besides lazily checking out the club—staring at the signs and bouncing a little to the music.

Suddenly Jean-Claude leaned down and whispered something to Bess. Bess nodded and looked around, and the two of them started walking toward the main exit.

They never got there. With silent efficiency, two of the masked men grabbed Bess from behind. Her eyes widened in shock. But she didn't have time to scream as they pulled her toward the wall.

Then all three of them melted into the darkness of the underground tunnel behind door number three.

Chapter

Eight

FRANK AND NANCY didn't have to exchange a word before they were off and flying across the dance floor. Joe must have sensed something was wrong. He broke away from his partner and was two steps behind them.

Jean-Claude was struggling with the two remaining men beside door three, but he was no match for them. He was pushed, stumbling, into the tunnel.

The heavy door was just about to swing shut behind them when Joe burst past Nancy and Frank to grab the handle. He tugged the door open and ran inside.

"Careful, Joe!" Nancy yelled. She plunged into the tunnel after him.

It was pitch-black inside. All the light bulbs must have been removed from their fixtures. Nancy ran blindly, her arms out in front of her, surrounded by darkness. Sounds of breathing and a jumble of footsteps echoed off the walls of the tunnel. Just ahead of her was the garbled sound of male voices. Was one of them Frank's? She knew she had entered the tunnel before him, but maybe he'd passed her. Maybe he'd caught up to—

With a thud, Nancy's hands hit a wall, bending back her index finger painfully. The tunnel had taken a sharp turn to the right. Nancy caught her breath and looked over to see the flickering beam of a flashlight in the distance.

"Yeeeaggghh!" a voice cried out. There were some grunts and a scuffling noise. The light began to weave wildly all over the tunnel, then came to rest in one bright stream on the ground. Nancy raced along the wall toward the flashlight. She bent for it—and smashed heads with someone who'd had the same idea.

But Nancy's fingers circled the cold metal first. She raised the light and shone it directly into two dark eyes surrounded by a black ski mask.

Cursing, the man lowered his head. This was just long enough for Nancy to flip him down to the ground on his back, where he lay stunned.

She raised the beam and aimed it down the tunnel. Joe was fighting madly against one of two other masked men. Bess screamed, and the second straight-armed her against the wall.

Nancy tore down the tunnel and reached out to Bess's attacker. She grabbed the back of his ski mask, pulling it around so that the eyeholes were in the back.

"Hey, what the—" the man cried out, flailing his arms helplessly as Nancy pulled on his arm and rolled him over.

Joe's opponent turned toward his partner momentarily—just enough time for Joe to deliver a quick uppercut to his jaw. The two men tumbled to the ground.

Just then there was a burst of light at the end of the tunnel. "Come on!" Nancy shouted. Then to Joe, "Where's Frank?"

"Probably ahead of us!" Joe shouted. "Let's go!"

Together they raced toward the light.

At the end of the tunnel was a metal staircase. From above, light poured down from a street lamp that shone through the half-open exit door. The door flapped open and shut as Jean-Claude stood struggling with the fourth masked man.

"Help!" Jean-Claude shouted, gripping the doorjamb to keep from being dragged out.

Nancy and Joe thudded up the stairs. "Let go of him! You're outnumbered!" Nancy called.

The man bellowed with laughter. "What are you going to do?" he said. "Stab me with your lipstick?" With a sudden gesture, he reached into his pocket, pulled out a knife, and pointed it straight at Nancy. "You lose, kids!" With his other hand, he tightened his grip around Jean-Claude's neck. "Come on, you wimp!"

He pushed back with his heel, knocking the door wide open. Jean-Claude let out a strangled cry as he was dragged outside.

From her position halfway up the stairs, Nancy couldn't see behind the man. But she did hear a dull thud.

The masked man reeled back into view, stood still for a second or two, looking down into the tunnel, then collapsed in a heap at the top of the stairs.

Nancy, Joe, and Bess dashed up the stairs as Jean-Claude began pounding his attacker.

But a pair of hands reached down and grabbed Jean-Claude's shoulders, pulling him outside. "Hey, take it easy. I just knocked the guy out!"

"Frank!" Nancy said incredulously. "How did you—"

Frank smiled. "Sometimes guidebooks are very useful—especially ones with maps of interesting underground tunnels. I remembered the location of the street exit, and figured I'd bring up the rear for you."

Jean-Claude straightened himself up. For the first time since they had met him, he looked afraid. He was shivering with more than the cold.

Tears welled up in Bess's eyes. "Jean-Claude!" she cried. "What did they do to you?" She ran out the door toward him, her arms outstretched.

But when she hugged him, he didn't respond.

He just stared straight ahead, then slowly his body slumped to the icy sidewalk.

"Quick!" Frank said. "Let's get him up." They dragged Jean-Claude over to a curb and sat him up.

"Look!" Nancy cried. "Over there!"

The three masked men staggered out of the main doorway a half block away and into a waiting car. It roared backward, plumes of exhaust filling the cold night air. Frank and Joe yanked Jean-Claude safely up onto the sidewalk, out of the car's path.

Just then Jean-Claude's attacker ran past them and dove through the open door into the backseat.

Joe followed the car for a few steps, realizing at once how useless it would be.

Bess was frantically fanning Jean-Claude's face with her hand. At last his eyes began to flicker. "Wha— Where—" he stammered.

"It's me, Jean-Claude. Bess!"

"Bess . . ." Jean-Claude moaned. Then he jerked wide-awake, his eyes full of panic. "Where are they? Help me!" he gasped.

"They're gone," Bess said softly. She gently raked her fingers through his hair. "Are you all right?"

Wordlessly, Jean-Claude rose to his feet, with Bess supporting him. She put her arm around his waist. Breathing deeply, Jean-Claude began walking with her toward his limo.

Nancy started to join them, but the abrupt,

gasping noises she heard suddenly made her stop. She wasn't positive, but she thought she heard Crown Prince Jean-Claude of Sarconne crying softly.

"How's Jean-Claude doing?" Frank asked as Bess and Nancy entered the Winslow's reading lounge to join the Hardy brothers.

"Fine," Nancy said. "Count Reynaud's with him."

"He may join us for hot cider," Bess said.

The two girls snuggled down into wine-colored leather wing chairs that were set in a fan shape in front of a roaring fireplace. The mantelpiece was heaped with pine boughs and circled with gold ribbons. A plate of Christmas cookies and some mugs of cider were on a small table in front of the foursome. Only a few other people were in the room—an old woman leafing through a magazine, a businessman reading a newspaper, a couple playing chess, and a gray-haired man whom they recognized as Fiona Fox's father.

Joe was staring into the fire, deep in thought. "I just can't figure who those guys could be," he said.

"Jean-Claude's theory about the cat burglars being the kidnappers has to be wrong," Frank remarked. "None of those four guys seemed younger than twenty-five or thirty."

"Just what I was thinking," Joe replied. "Looks like we have another case on our hands."

"You know, as bodyguards we really should

stick by him," Bess warned. "He was so shaken by this."

"Mm-hm," Nancy said, leaning forward in her chair. "Unlike the first kidnapping."

Frank watched her with a bemused expression. "You're right. He came out of that one as cool and confident as ever."

"And this time he fell apart," Nancy continued.

Bess looked at them indignantly. "What are you saying?"

"Nothing," Nancy said with a shrug. "Just observing the details."

"I can't believe you!" Bess said. "I mean, Jean-Claude could have been killed! It doesn't sound as though anyone really cares!"

"I'm sorry, Bess," Nancy said gently. "I know it must have been awful for both of you."

"What happened exactly?" Joe asked. "Those guys just appeared out of nowhere?"

Bess sat back in her chair. "Well, we didn't actually see them until we were almost out the exit—"

"Wait a minute," Joe interrupted. "Almost out the exit? Were you leaving?"

Bess's face turned red. "Well, yes. Jean-Claude wanted to—"

This time Nancy cut her off. "Bess, you *knew* we were all supposed to stay together! Why didn't you at least tell us?"

"I tried! But, well, you know Jean-Claude."

As Bess spoke, Frank and Joe felt someone

enter the room and glanced over at the doorway behind Nancy. Nancy turned too. Jean-Claude was moving toward them. He was wearing new designer jeans, a blue-and-white-striped cotton shirt, and a blue V-necked sweater. His hair was slicked back, wet, and the only reminder of his fight was a small bandage on his forehead. Entering just after him and remaining at the door were his two bodyguards.

Frank pulled another chair into their semicircle.

"Thank you," Jean-Claude said with a small smile. "And thanks for rescuing me—twice—today. I am in debt to you."

"No problem," Joe said as Jean-Claude sat down. He held out the plate of cookies. "Have some before I finish them."

"I will," Jean-Claude said, taking three. "I'm starving!"

He sounds like himself again, Nancy thought. "Do you have any idea who those men were?" she asked.

"Do you think it might have been the same people who kidnapped you outside the Met?" Frank added.

"No," Jean-Claude snapped back. "Absolutely not."

"How do you know?" Joe said. "They were wearing masks."

"I know because the pair that took me outside the Met was a duo. Also one of the people was much older."

84

"To tell you the truth, *I* don't think they were after Jean-Claude," Bess interjected. "I mean, they went for *me* first. They only grabbed Jean-Claude when he tried to stop them."

Frank drummed his fingers on the arm of his chair. "There's got to be a connection we're all missing here," he said in a frustrated voice. "We should be able to figure this out."

"I'll get our notes," Joe said. He trotted out of the room and headed for the elevators.

Jean-Claude sighed and leaned his head against the high back of the wing chair. The room fell silent, except for the crackling of the fire. One log collapsed into a glowing shower of embers as they watched. Soon some of the other people in the room began leaving—first the old woman, then Fiona's father, then the couple.

"We chased them all away," Bess said with a laugh, looking around at the room. "They heard us and thought we were crazy."

"I don't know about that," Jean-Claude said softly, with a rakish smile. "Maybe they were blinded by the two fires in the room."

"Two?" Bess said curiously. "There's only one fireplace."

"You have forgotten the fire of your incredible beauty."

Bess giggled. "Oh, stop it."

Nancy couldn't help cringing a little. Don't you recognize a line when you hear it? she wanted to ask Bess. You shouldn't fall for him so easily!

But she didn't say anything to Bess. *This case is going nowhere fast,* she reminded herself glumly. *The last thing I need is to lose one of my two best friends in the bargain.*

Joe was lost in thought as he turned the key to his and Frank's room. Something was a little off about this whole case, but he couldn't quite put his finger on it. How many people were really after Jean-Claude? Why had the masked men gone after Bess first? And why were there four of them?

The questions raced through Joe's mind as he pushed the door open and stepped into the dark foyer. The light from the hallway illuminated the wall enough for him to see the light switch. He reached for it as the door swung closed.

Suddenly he felt his body being jerked back. A black-gloved hand covered his mouth.

The room plunged into total darkness as the door clicked shut behind him.

"Back so soon?" a voice whispered.

The last thing Joe felt was an unbearable pain from a crack on his skull, and then the room burst into an explosion of swirling stars and red dots. Joe toppled forward as the floor rushed up to meet him.

Chapter

Nine

Whaт's тaking Joe so long?" Frank wondered out loud, staring at the chessboard in front of him. Absentmindedly he moved his queen to avoid being taken by Nancy's bishop.

"I was wondering the same thing," Nancy answered. "Maybe he decided to write down what we were talking about while it was still fresh in his memory. Oh, by the way . . ."

She moved her knight to within striking distance of Frank's king. She was amazed he'd left himself so wide open that early in the game. "Check!" she said with a triumphant smile.

From a leather couch on the other side of the room came a playful squeal. "Oh, Jean-Claude!"

"I can't believe she's fallen for him so hard," Nancy said. She stole a look and saw Jean-Claude massaging Bess's shoulders. Quickly she looked away.

"To tell you the truth," Frank answered in a low voice, "I'm a little worried. She's so totally out of her skull about Jean-Claude. I mean, suppose he's trying to pull something on us. Would Bess take his side or ours?" He moved his king.

"I wouldn't worry about that, Frank. Bess would never do anything to hurt us." Nancy gave Frank a reassuring smile. She only wished she could quiet the voice inside her that was saying maybe Frank was right.

"I guess I'm feeling frustrated," Frank said. "We're nowhere, and tomorrow the jewels will be at the U.N."

Suddenly Nancy's eyes flared, and she made a quick move with her rook. "Checkmate!" She couldn't believe it. She'd actually beaten Frank in eight moves! Grinning, she looked up for his reaction.

But Frank was only gazing blankly at the board. "This really isn't like Joe. I'm going to get him." He got up from the table. "Make sure nobody touches the board. I'll make my move when I get back."

"But the game is—" It was too late. Frank was out the door. Nancy sighed. She'd have to be the only one to appreciate her victory.

* * *

The door was ajar when Frank got to the room. "Joe?" he called out, pushing it open.

"Ohhhhhh!" Joe moaned in response. "Turn that light off!"

Frank felt a rush of anger. "You fell *asleep* while we were all downstairs waiting?" he snapped. He stepped inside, ready to wring his brother's neck.

Just then, a man stepped out of the bathroom, holding a bag of ice. It was Fiona Fox's father!

"What are *you* doing here?" Frank said.

"Sssssh!" the man replied. "He's still a little sensitive to loud noises"—he reached past Frank and turned the dimmer switch—"and bright lights."

Frank walked through the foyer into the room, completely confused.

"Frank?" Joe called out weakly.

Frank's eyes widened as he took in his brother stretched out on the bed with an ice bag on his forehead. "Joe! What happened?"

Joe tried to sit up, but immediately fell back. The gray-haired man eased the pillow under his head and changed the ice bag. "Not yet, young man," he said.

"Thanks, Dr. Fox," Joe said. He looked up at Frank. "I—I was ambushed, Frank. As soon as I opened the door, somebody whacked me over the head. I'd still be on the floor now if Dr. Fox hadn't come along."

Dr. Fox smiled politely and extended a hand to Frank. "Trevor Fox. I believe we met informally in the lobby. Your brother was, uh, photographing my daughter."

"Unfortunately, she's out seeing a show," Joe added. Then he smiled shakily. "Otherwise maybe she'd be up here, too."

Trevor Fox chuckled. "Anyway, your brother is a lucky young fellow. Fiona and I are staying just down the hall, and I was on my way there when I noticed that the door to this room was ajar. Well, at first I thought nothing of it and walked right past. But then I heard a moan. I came back, pushed open the door—and there was Joe, lying on the floor."

"Did you call a doctor?" Frank asked.

"I *am* a doctor," Fox said. "Retired but still effective. All Joe needs is ice and a good night's rest. I'm sure he'll be fine in the morning." He pointed to the dresser. "There's a pile of plastic bags. There are two buckets of ice in the bathtub. Now I'm afraid I must bid you gentlemen good night." With that, he walked toward the door.

"Good night, Dr. Fox," Frank called out. "And thanks."

"By the way," Dr. Fox said, turning back toward them, "the intruder made a bit of a mess—he went through the closets and drawers. I tidied up, but I think you ought to check to see if anything was stolen."

The door shut behind Dr. Fox, and Frank sat beside Joe on the bed. "Did you get a look at who did it?" he asked.

Joe shook his head. "It was totally dark, and he

had me from behind. All I know is that he was tall and had a voice like this . . ." He did an imitation of a whispery voice saying, "Back so soon?"

"Hmm. Someone's been keeping an eye on our whereabouts." Frank exhaled and gave Joe a meaningful look.

"I know what you're thinking," Joe said. "I caught the cat burglars in the act. But it doesn't make sense—why would they be robbing *our* room?"

"The photos!" Frank exclaimed, getting up. "Maybe they found out about them—"

"I thought of that. They're still on the dresser," Joe interrupted.

Frank sat back down. "Maybe you got here just in time—before they were found. I guess we were lucky."

Joe groaned and adjusted his ice bag. "Yeah, Frank. I feel like the luckiest guy in the world."

"What did you find out about those photos?" Nancy called into the bathroom, where Bess was putting on makeup the next morning.

No answer.

"Bess?" Nancy walked over to the bathroom and observed Bess smiling at herself in the mirror. "Bess—what are you doing?" she asked.

Bess's face reddened, and she quickly turned around. "Oh, uh, nothing. Just—"

"Did you hear my question?"

"What question?"

"What did you find out about those photos of father-son duos I gave you? You know, the ones that Joe took? You were supposed to find out about them from Winslow security," she added, trying to jog Bess's memory.

"Oh, no," Bess moaned, covering her face with her hand. "I got sidetracked. All I wanted to do was get Jean-Claude a little present, but—"

"So you forgot, didn't you?"

Bess nodded.

Nancy leaned against the bathroom wall and met Bess's gaze in the mirror. "Bess, I know how you feel about Jean-Claude. I mean, let's face it—he is gorgeous and a lot of fun. But remember, we're here for a reason." Bess looked so guilty that Nancy couldn't hold back a smile. "Look, I'm not telling you to stop having a good time," she said more gently. "All I'm saying is that we have a job to do. The U.N. party is *tonight.* You know, I'm still trying to figure out how Jean-Claude talked us into going ice-skating at lunchtime."

"I really am sorry, Nancy," Bess said. "Look, I promise I'll show those photos to the security people this morning. They'll tell us right away who these people are. And I promise I won't let Jean-Claude talk me into doing anything irresponsible again." She held up three fingers. "Girl Scouts' honor."

Nancy laughed. "Okay, Bess. I didn't mean to nag. I'm just a little tense about this case."

"Come on," Bess answered cheerfully. She

picked up the photos and pulled her coat from the closet.

"Are you sure you're all right?" Bess reached across the table toward Jean-Claude, who'd taken a spill on the Rockefeller Center rink moments before.

Jean-Claude encircled her hand with his and grinned. "Now I am." Across from Nancy, Joe reached gloomily for his cup of hot chocolate as he tried to ignore Bess and Jean-Claude. He looked as if he were about to explode.

Time for a little distraction, Nancy thought. "This really is a gorgeous place, isn't it, Joe?" she said loudly. She gestured toward the enormous window along one wall of the restaurant. Outside the window, skaters glided by. Above them, the huge Rockefeller Center Christmas tree stretched up eight stories, twinkling with thousands of lights.

"You looked so cute sitting there on the ice," Bess said with a giggle.

"Oh, well," Jean-Claude replied, his face growing red. "I knew I shouldn't stare at you, but watch where I was going."

Joe slammed his cup down on the table. "Don't you two ever knock it off?" he snapped.

Jean-Claude and Bess stared at him in shocked silence.

"That's more like it," Joe grumbled. "Better than listening to you, anyway."

Bess's eyes were blazing. She opened her

mouth to answer, but before she could say anything, Jean-Claude stood up quickly. "Well, Bess, I feel pretty good now! Let's give it another try!" he said.

He grabbed her hand and pulled her toward the door. The two of them disappeared, leaving Nancy, Frank, and Joe alone at the table.

Frank shook his head. "Great, Joe. Open your mouth and set them against us! That's just what we need right now!"

Joe pushed himself back from the table and stood up. "Look, I've had just about enough. We've been asked here by the chief of police of New York City to try to find out who these cat burglars are, and instead we end up dealing with Prince Charming and Cinderella. I have to be the bodyguard of someone who likes to climb out of windows all the time, and I get cracked over the head for no reason at all. Then my own brother tells me off! I'm out of here!"

He turned and stalked away.

Frank and Nancy looked at each other awkwardly across the table. "Maybe I shouldn't have said anything," Frank said.

"No," Nancy answered with a deep sigh. "This was bound to happen sometime."

She tried to feel optimistic, but it wasn't easy. They were nowhere close to solving the case— they didn't even have one new lead. Time was running out. And now the detectives weren't even speaking to each other.

As the Christmas music tinkled through the restaurant, Nancy put her elbows on the table and propped her head up in her hands. "Merry Christmas, everyone," she muttered bleakly. She wished that she could think of an answer besides "Bah, humbug!"

Chapter

Ten

W<small>ELL, AT LEAST</small> they didn't skip out on us this time," Frank said, gazing out into the rink.

Nancy leaned forward on the low wall separating the skaters from the spectators. She was feeling better after leaving the restaurant. "For once Jean-Claude's making it easy for us to keep an eye on him," she remarked.

She watched as Bess skated arm in arm with Jean-Claude. Despite the trouble Bess had been causing, Nancy couldn't help but smile. The two of them looked so happy. Who was she to deny her best friend?

Frank moved over and stood next to Nancy.

"You never told me what you found out about those photos. Any progress?"

Nancy shook her head. "Bess checked them with security—about ten father-son combos. Most of the fathers are established businessmen —their sons on vacation from college. In almost all the cases, the mothers and other siblings are along, too."

"Doesn't sound too promising."

"No," Nancy agreed. "But I did see something interesting in today's paper. It seems that this U.N. gala is not only to celebrate Sarconne's five-hundredth anniversary, it's also to welcome them officially to the U.N."

"Welcome them?" Frank said. "I thought they were already in."

"There was a verbal agreement by the king many years ago, and some informal relations were set up. But there was a very strong faction in Sarconne that opposed membership. Many members of the upper class were in that faction, including our friend Reynaud. But a rumor spread that these same leaders wanted to set up a dictatorship. And the other members of the faction wouldn't hear of it—they were afraid of losing their holdings. So the opposition to joining the U.N. began to dissolve."

"And now Jean-Claude is going to sign some official papers?"

"Right. His father couldn't come. His health is quite fragile. Anyway, the signing takes place after the dinner."

Frank grimaced. "Unless everyone is busy searching for the stolen jewels by then."

Suddenly Frank stiffened. A powerful hand had grabbed him by the shoulder. He spun around, his fists clenched.

"Hey, easy. I didn't get you *that* mad, did I?"

It was Joe—smiling broadly as if the earlier argument had never happened. "How come you two wallflowers aren't on the ice?"

It didn't take long to see what had caused the change in Joe. Walking up beside him, skates slung over her shoulder, was Fiona Fox.

"Hello. I don't think we've met," she said to Nancy and Frank with her melodious British accent. She tossed back her silken auburn hair. Her warm smile revealed two rows of perfect, white teeth.

Joe introduced them all. Then he and Fiona sat down to put on their skates and then immediately went onto the rink, skating in graceful circles beneath the towering Christmas tree.

Nancy gazed back and forth between the two couples: Bess and Jean-Claude, Joe and Fiona. Each of them seemed to glow with a special light no one else shared. The radiant smiles, the giddy laughter—it was as if each couple was in its own orbit, miles from the other people on the rink.

A warm feeling spread through Nancy. If only Ned were here . . . She imagined herself gliding across the rink, looking up into those wonderful eyes—

All of a sudden Nancy realized it wasn't Ned's eyes she was imagining. It was . . .

Immediately she became conscious of Frank's presence beside her. And hard as she tried, she couldn't control the rush of blood to her face. She just knew she was turning beet red.

He's going to notice this, she thought. He's going to ask me what's wrong. What am I going to tell him?

But if Frank did notice, he didn't let on. Instead, he kept staring at the rink, not saying a word.

Finally, in a soft, almost shy voice, he said, "Looks like the four of them are having fun."

Nancy nodded wordlessly.

"Maybe we ought to . . ." Frank let his voice trail off.

"Ought to what?" Nancy asked.

Frank turned to look at her only inches from him. Nancy could feel his brown eyes searching her face. "You know, I've been doing some thinking, Nancy."

Doing some thinking. I don't believe he's saying this, Nancy thought. Her heart was pounding wildly.

Just then a roar went up from the crowd. Nancy and Frank glanced around.

Silently, lazily, the first snowfall of the year had begun. Thick, meandering flakes landed on hats and shoulders as children reached up eagerly to catch them. Even the stodgiest-looking people on the rink were grinning and chatting with their partners.

"Merry Christmas!" Frank said to Nancy.

"Merry Christmas," Nancy answered. Was Frank going to finish what he had started to say?

She looked at him casually, trying not to show what was racing through her head. But Frank's eyes were now fixed on something at the far end of the rink.

Nancy followed his gaze. There, leaning against the low wall were Joe and a man. They were locked in some sort of argument.

Something about the man was familiar. Nancy watched him carefully until he turned around.

The shock of recognition hit her and Frank at the same time. It was the chestnut vendor who had kidnapped Jean-Claude!

"Come on! We have to get out there!" Frank said.

The two of them pushed toward the rink's entrance. They stepped onto the ice, but were stopped abruptly. A tall, burly rink guard looked down at Frank scornfully. "Ho-o-old on a minute, buddy! No one's allowed on the ice without skates. Understand?"

Before the man had even finished speaking, Frank and Nancy dashed back into the rental desk. Thank heaven! Nancy thought. No line.

"Size eight!" she said breathlessly.

"Ten!" Frank added.

The woman behind the desk looked up at them with heavy-lidded eyes. Sighing wearily, she put down the crossword puzzle she'd been working on. Then she strolled slowly back to the shoe racks, carefully examining her nail polish.

Nancy felt like screaming at her.

The woman returned empty-handed. "Those sizes are all out. If you want to wait until somebody comes back—"

Frantically Nancy looked around. Piled up on the floor beside the woman was a stack of returned skates that hadn't been reshelved. Nancy pointed to a pair on top. "I'll take those!" she said.

"Those?" The woman stared at Nancy as if she were crazy. "But you don't know what size they are. You want me to look?"

Frank slapped some money down on the counter. "Just give them to her!" he ordered. "And give me that blue pair!"

The woman rolled her eyes. "All right, take your chances. But there are no refunds."

Frank and Nancy grabbed the skates and pulled them on. Nancy's were way too big, so she yanked the laces as tight as she could. Then they hobbled back out to the rink.

Nancy could see Joe waving his arms furiously at the man. The rink guard was now between them, trying to stop the argument. And against the wall stood Fiona, looking anxious and bewildered.

Frank barged through the opening with Nancy close behind.

But no sooner had she set foot on the ice than someone grabbed her arm and began tugging violently on it.

Chapter

Eleven

Help! Frank!" Nancy screamed. She was speeding along on the ice, almost out of control. Someone had a crushingly strong grip on her arm. She tried to pull loose, but it was impossible. Her skates made a *ski-i-ish* sound as they cut an edge through the ice. Skaters scattered as she approached. She looked up to see the wall of the rink rushing closer. She'd crash into it . . . But at the last second she was yanked away from the wall—her arm feeling longer by two inches.

Only then did Nancy realize what was happening. A long chain of people were stretched across the rink, all holding hands. Nancy's half of the chain was facing one way; the other half was facing the opposite way. The line was moving in a circle, like a pinwheel, so that the last people had to skate furiously to keep up with the momentum.

Snap-the-whip! Nancy thought with relief. It was a game she'd played in River Heights as a little girl.

A shrill whistle pierced the air, and the rink guard shouted, "Break it up! You can't do that here!"

There were a few groans, but in a second the line had broken up. The guy who'd been holding Nancy's arm smiled at her as he skated off. As the "whip" dispersed, Frank skated to Nancy's side. "Come on!" he said, taking her hand himself.

The two of them skated away at top speed, but when they got to the spot where Joe had been, no one was there.

Nancy stared blankly around the rink. Joe, Fiona, and the chestnut vendor were nowhere to be seen.

Frank's face was taut with anxiety. Nancy knew that the same thing was on both their minds. Could Joe have been taken by the kidnapper?

"Let's get rid of our skates," Frank said abruptly.

Seconds later they were back at the skate-rental counter, where the woman was methodically putting skates away. "Did you see three people just leave?" Frank asked her breathlessly. "A blond guy and an auburn-haired girl about eighteen, with a kind of tough-looking older guy?"

"Oh, so *you're* the brother," she said, a smile of faint recognition creasing her face as she scrutinized Frank.

"You mean you saw him?" Frank broke in.

"Yeah. He told me you'd be looking for him. He and his girlfriend left in kind of a hurry—she looked upset. I didn't notice any older guy, though."

"Did he say anything else to you?" Frank pressed. "Did he mention where he was going?"

"Uh-huh. He told me to tell you something." She scrunched her face up, trying to remember. "He said he'd meet you in an hour at . . . uh . . . I forget."

Nancy could see that Frank was about to explode. "Was it a street corner? A building?" she cut in. "Did he give you an address?"

"No, no . . ." The woman tapped her fingers on the counter. "It was some store, I think. Macy's, Bloomingdale's, Saks, something like—"

"Saks! Of course!" Nancy said. "That's where Bess wanted to go after skating."

"Yeah, Saks. That was it!" the woman agreed, her face brightening.

"Thanks a lot," Frank said. "He didn't say where he was going in the meantime, did he?"

"No, but as they headed out the door he was saying something about seeing the sights. If you ask me, they probably just wanted to run around the city a little." She grinned. "Nice couple."

Nancy and Frank went back to the side of the rink. Bess and Jean-Claude whizzed by, and Bess waved merrily.

"Look at it this way, Frank," Nancy said. "Jean-Claude is safe for the time being, one kidnapper, at least, is out of sight. And the others wouldn't dare pull anything here in broad daylight."

Frank made a little half bow for Nancy to enter. "I guess that means I have an hour to show you a little something about skating."

"Oh, we'll see about *that!*" Nancy said, her feet sliding around in her oversized skates. With a mischievous gleam in her eyes, she took off onto the ice, Frank right behind her.

"It's absolutely remarkable, how you've transformed this bathroom," Fiona Fox said, staring amazed at the gadgets and trays that Joe had set up on folding tables. "You must be a professional photographer!"

Joe flashed a cocky smile. "No, not exactly. Let's just say I'm a jack-of-all-trades. Anyway, I figure that if you need photos developed in hurry, you've got to do them yourself!"

Fiona laughed. "I suppose so. Although I'd think one of those twenty-four-hour photo labs would be perfectly adequate."

Perfectly adequate. If Joe had heard anyone else his age use those words, he would immediately have thought *total nerd*. But somehow it sounded unbelievably sexy in that British accent and soft, deep voice. Not to mention those incredible flashing eyes—and that hair! He had a new mission now: to make Fiona think he was the most exciting man she had ever met—and to do it before Jean-Claude noticed her.

"Perfectly adequate!" Joe scoffed. "Not if you only photograph subjects of the utmost beauty and complexity—the way I do!" Not bad, Joe said to himself, surprised at his choice of words.

"Well!" Fiona said with a throaty laugh. When she tossed her hair back, it fell into perfect, lustrous waves. "I guess you'll have to show me one of those beautiful, complex subjects."

Joe led her out into the bedroom. Fortunately, Bess had put the photos back on top of his dresser before going to the rink. He searched through the stack. "Let's see," he said, pulling one out. "I think you'll recognize the person in this one."

He'd only managed to take one photo of Fiona, but it was a beauty. There she was, leaning over the balcony, surveying the grand lobby of the Winslow as if she owned it. All the guests around her, both men and women, seemed to be staring at her.

"Oh, that's lovely!" Fiona exclaimed. She laughed and immediately added, "If I do say so myself. What a wonderful candid photographer you are!"

Joe felt incredibly pleased with himself. "Well,

I think photography is more instinctive than anything else. Of course, the lighting must be—"

"Such excellent contours and depth," Fiona bubbled on. "I suspect you were using ambient light and a rather fast film—ASA four hundred at least. And yet the grain is so fine!"

"Uh, yes. Yes, that's right." Joe was floored. *She knows more about this stuff than I do!* he thought.

"Interesting interplay between the horizontals and verticals. Good, deep depth of field. Oh, I hope this isn't your only copy. I'd love to keep it."

"Well, it *is* my only copy." Joe smiled warmly, trying to seem as if he hadn't been flustered by Fiona's expertise. "But I meant it for you."

"Oh, thank you!" Fiona said excitedly. "I can't wait to show my father. I'm sure he'll want one, too!"

Joe could sense opportunity knocking— loudly. "Really? Hey, no problem!" he said. "I'll make him one right now in the darkroom. Would you like to join me?"

"May I? I've never actually been in a darkroom before."

That sounded a little strange, coming from someone who knew so much about photography, but Joe wasn't about to argue. His plan was working perfectly.

"Well, it'll be a little crowded, but why not?" Joe pulled a negative out of an envelope and held it up to the light. There were six images on it; one of them was the picture of Fiona. Holding it carefully by the edges, he walked to the bathroom and opened the door. "If you'll just step all the way in, I'll close the door. We need, uh, total darkness for this."

"Oh, how exciting!" Fiona replied with a little shiver.

Joe turned off the overhead light. Now only a dim red light shone in the room—a so-called safe light, the kind that wouldn't disturb the developing pictures. It bathed the room in a soft, romantic red glow. Perfect.

Quickly Joe mapped out the strategy in his head. First he would develop the photo, impressing Fiona with his darkroom know-how. The last step was a ten-minute "bath" for the print in a pan of water. For that ten minutes, they'd have nothing to do—in the dark, quiet, *intimate* room, with the soft red light. Foolproof.

Joe flicked on the enlarger nonchalantly. An image of the picture beamed down onto the photographic paper for a few seconds.

"That looks dreadful!" Fiona said.

"It's the negative image," Joe replied. "Watch what happens when I put it in this developer." He took the paper and immersed it in a pan full of clear liquid. Slowly the photograph began to emerge.

In the dead silence of the room, Joe could hear Fiona breathing. The only other sound was the steady pounding of his heart, which boomed louder by the second.

But then there was another sound—a tiny, muted click outside the darkroom door.

"That's just fascinating, Joe. I—"

"Sssh!" Joe cut her off. "Did you hear that?"

"What?"

Click. There it was again. It was coming from the door to the suite. "Someone's trying to get in," he whispered. "Just stay here and don't make a sound."

He moved to the darkroom door and listened. The clicking got quicker and louder, and before long he could hear the squeak of a door opening.

My old cat burglar friend, Joe thought. I'll be the one to surprise him this time. He waited until he heard the door swing shut, until the intruder was completely inside the front foyer.

"Joe, be careful!" Fiona called in a frightened voice.

There was no waiting now. The intruder must have heard that voice.

With lightning-quick reflexes, Joe flung the door open.

But the man had been warned; he had the foyer light out and had broken away to run out the front door.

Joe raced after him into the hallway and followed him down an emergency stairwell. The sound of their footsteps echoed loudly against the rough concrete walls and treads. As Joe spiraled downward, his eyes caught the floor numbers painted in red on the gray walls: 4—3—2—

Suddenly the stairwell became silent. Joe cautiously took the stairs two at a time to the first floor. He turned to go down to the basement.

Fooooosh! Stopping on the first-floor landing, Joe dove to the floor just as a cloud of white foam burst up at him from the basement.

A fire extinguisher, Joe realized. This guy wasn't stupid.

There was a clanking sound, and the blast stopped. Joe grabbed onto the railing, and lowered himself carefully down the slick, foam-coated treads to the basement floor. But by the time he got there, the man was long gone.

Joe stared through the door into the long, empty hallways of the Winslow basement. Then, with a long sigh, he turned and trudged back up to the fifth floor. As he walked along, he wiped off the traces of fire-extinguisher fluid from the bottom of his pants. Luckily, he'd jumped away in time to avoid being doused—but that was the *only* lucky thing about all this.

The suite door was ajar when Joe returned. He pushed it open glumly, half expecting Fiona to be gone.

And he was right. Great! he thought. I scared her away. Just when things were—

"Help! Joe, is that you?"

The muffled voice was Fiona's! Joe ran into the bedroom.

"I'm in the closet! Please help me!"

Joe grabbed the doorknob, but it wouldn't budge. The key! Where was the closet key? He ran to the dresser and looked under stacks of papers, photos, souvenirs. No key. He looked back at the closet door, trying to figure out how he could break it.

That's when he saw the key. It was lying on the carpet by the closet door in plain sight.

Joe scooped it up and opened the door. Fiona practically fell out into his arms. "Oh, Joe!" she gasped.

Carefully Joe picked her up and set her down on the bed. "Are you all right?" he asked.

"As soon as you left," Fiona said breathlessly, "a man came into the darkroom. I screamed— He threw me in the closet. Ohhhh! I'm so glad you came back!"

Into the darkroom? He couldn't let himself think about that yet. "You just lie back and relax, Fiona. You'll be all right," Joe said reassuringly.

He quickly punched a number on the hotel phone. "Hello, Dr. Fox? This is Joe Hardy. Please come over right away. Fiona's been a little shaken up." He hung up and turned to Fiona. "He'll be right over," he told her.

Then he rushed into the darkroom. The first thing he noticed was the photo he'd been developing. It had been exposed to light and was now pitch-black.

Then Joe noticed the negatives were gone!

Chapter

Twelve

THERE, THERE, LOVE. Just sit back and sip this."
Dr. Fox held a cup of hot tea to his daughter's
lips.

"I'm fine, Father," Fiona said, sitting up on the
edge of the bed. "Really."

"Would you like me to order something else
from room service?" Joe asked. "Juice, some
lunch—"

"No, thank you," Fiona answered firmly.
"I—I think I'd just like to leave now and go to
my room."

Joe nodded. "Of course. I understand." Just
what I need, he thought. I finally meet the girl of

my dreams, and I have to drag her into this ridiculous case.

"Come, darling," Dr. Fox said, putting his arm around Fiona's shoulder to help her up.

The two of them walked haltingly to the door. "Goodbye, Joe. I'll see you around, I'm sure," Fiona said—without looking back at him.

As the door closed behind them, Joe slumped down onto the bed. He felt as if the whole world had fallen apart. All the photos of possible suspects were gone. How was he going to explain it to Frank and Nancy?

But that wasn't the worst part. Worst of all was losing Fiona Fox—just as things were starting to happen between them. How could life get worse?

All it took was a glance at his watch to find his answer. It was ten minutes to two. He was supposed to have met Frank and Nancy twenty minutes earlier.

Grabbing his coat, Joe dashed out the door, slamming it behind him.

"Silver bells, silver bells,
It's Christmastime in the city!"

The carol blared from speakers overhead as Nancy, Jean-Claude, and Bess peered into the store window. Miniature motorized men in top hats and women in bustles walked choppily back and forth along a nineteenth-century city street, holding presents and waving to each other. A sign above them said: Christmas on Fifth Avenue, 1890.

Nancy turned and peered through the crowds in search of Frank. Finally she saw him standing out by the curb near a skinny man in a Santa suit, wearing a beard that looked like cotton candy.

"Frank, come see this window! It's great!" Nancy called out.

Frank smiled wanly and nodded. "I will," he called back in a dispirited voice. But he just brushed the falling snowflakes from his face and looked up and down the street.

With a slow, rhythmic *clop, clop, clop,* two horse-drawn carriages pulled up to the front of the store, just past the crowd. "Coach rides? Coach rides through the park, anyone?" called one of the drivers.

"Ah," Jean-Claude said. "Our coachmen are waiting!" He took Bess's hand, fluttered a quick wave to his bodyguards, and pushed through the crowd toward the horses.

"Come on, guys!" Bess called. "This'll be fun!"

Nancy's face lit up. "Oh, let's go, Frank!" she begged, walking up to him. "It'll only take a few minutes."

"Uh, no—you go ahead with them," Frank said, looking at his watch. "I'm going to stick around and wait for Joe. He was supposed to be here a half hour ago."

"Don't worry," Nancy said. "I'm sure he and Fiona are off in their own world somewhere.

Right about now they're probably realizing how late they are."

A grin inched its way across Frank's face as he spotted something down the street. "I guess you're right," he said.

Nancy turned to follow his glance. About a block away, Joe was sprinting toward them, dodging in and out of shoppers like a fullback.

"Frank! Nancy!" Joe called. He ran up to them, panting. "Listen, I'm sorry I'm late, but—"

"Save it for the ride, Joe," Frank said. "Judging from the look of the horses, we're going to have plenty of time."

"What?"

Frank gestured over to where Jean-Claude and Bess had been standing.

"I still don't get it, Frank."

Frank turned around. Jean-Claude and Bess were gone. "Where are—" he began.

Slowly one of the carriages pulled away from the curb. Jean-Claude's head popped out of the side. "Joe! You're here!" he called out. "Get in the other carriage with Nancy and Frank! And tell my guards I'll be right back."

"Last one to Central Park gets coal in his stocking!" Bess added as their horse entered a lane of traffic.

"Come on! Let's go!" Frank said, blocking the bodyguards so they couldn't get in the last carriage. "I don't want them out of our sight!"

The three of them climbed in and told the driver to "follow that horse."

Solemn-faced joggers and speeding taxis passed by as the horses trotted leisurely through the park. The sound of tinkling music from a carousel mixed with the squeals of children playing in the snow nearby.

But Nancy, snuggled down deep in two plaid blankets, barely noticed their surroundings. Joe was telling his story, and that was all she could think about.

"Well, I guess it's pretty obvious who would be interested in getting those negatives," Frank said after a long, discouraged silence when Joe had finished talking.

Joe nodded. "The burglars," he said glumly. "They must have been tipped off that I was taking photos."

"I just don't understand it, though," Nancy said. "I mean, yes, the burglars must have broken into your room just now—but what about the other two break-ins? First they ransacked *our* room. Why would they have been looking for the photos in there if they knew *Joe* was the photographer?"

"Good question," Frank said. "And when they did break into our room last night, why didn't they take the photos and negatives then? Everything was in plain sight on the dresser."

"But today must have been the first time the burglars broke in," Nancy said.

"What? I don't follow," Frank said.

"Well, didn't we decide that there are two groups. The cat burglars are after the jewels. And someone else is trying to kidnap Jean-Claude. Maybe the kidnappers are the ones who broke in those other times. They may be trying to send us a message to stay clear of Jean-Claude."

"That makes sense," Frank said. "If the kidnappers tracked us to the Underground, they could easily have tracked us to the hotel."

"But who are these guys? And how are they able to keep such close tabs on us?" Nancy asked. "If they just wanted to give us a warning, why did they go through all our drawers and closets?"

She stopped to think about that. "That's the big question. We must have something that they need. If only we could figure out what, we might be able to break this case wide open! At least one of them."

Nancy stared at Frank. Frank stared at Joe.

Joe shrugged. "I'm still stuck on who the cat burglars are." He shook his head, deep in thought. "I could have sworn none of those father-son teams noticed me!"

The carriage fell silent except for the bells on the horse's harness. Nancy shivered with cold as they passed a secluded area of cement chess tables and attached benches. Abandoned in the freezing cold, the tables stood silent watch, encrusted with snow and icicles.

Suddenly the answer was too clear to ignore. It had been nagging at her for a while, but she kept dismissing it. And she knew Joe wouldn't want to hear it. "There was one team that noticed you, Joe," she said quietly.

"You said you gave Fiona the photo you took of her," Nancy went on. "Was that the only copy you had?"

"Yes." A cloud seemed to pass across Joe's eyes, and he slumped back against the seat.

"And then she asked you to get the negative out and make another copy?"

"No," Joe answered. "I—I volunteered to do it myself."

"So, the father-son team—"

"Is actually a father-*daughter* team," Nancy said. "Fiona and Dr. Fox must have staged the theft of the negatives. Locking Fiona in the closet was a smoke screen—a way for them to appear innocent."

Joe shook his head. "I don't know, Nancy—"

"That's got to be it. You didn't see what happened after you left the Winslow's reading lounge last night, Joe," Nancy said. "Dr. Fox left right after you. And he was within earshot the whole time we were talking about the case beforehand."

Joe shook his head. "First of all, the guy who mugged me didn't have Fox's voice," he said. "Second, why didn't Dr. Fox take the photos then? Why did he stick around?"

"Because he was *planning* to break in, but the kidnappers got there first!" Nancy said excitedly. "It was a convenient coincidence for him. He probably waited for them to leave and went in afterward to take the photos—"

"Then we showed up, and he covered by flipping into his kindly doctor routine," Frank said.

Joe's blue eyes were flashing with rage. "When I get my hands on—"

Frank pounded the side of the carriage in frustration. "We've got to get back right away. Fiona and her father must have known that we'd figure all this out eventually. I wouldn't be surprised if they're checking out right now!"

"Sir!" Nancy said to the driver, leaning forward in her seat. "We've got to get to the Winslow Hotel immediately! Can you signal the other carriage?" She pointed up the road.

"What other carriage?" the driver replied.

Nancy's eyes opened in shock. Jean-Claude and Bess's carriage had disappeared!

"They were just in front of us!" she cried.

"I see them!" Joe said. "Way up ahead, on that hill."

In the distance Nancy saw the other horse pulling the carriage up the hill at a gallop. "What's going on? Is this one of Jean-Claude's crazy ideas? We've got to catch up to them!"

"Lady, I'll do the best I can," the driver answered in a monotone. He pulled on the reins.

The horse shifted into a lazy canter. "Hey, it's been a long time since the Kentucky Derby," the driver said with a chuckle. "She can't handle the occasional patches of ice."

"Never mind! Stop the carriage, please," Nancy said, handing the driver his fee. "Come on, guys. We're going to have to do this on foot!"

The three of them tossed off their blankets, jumped out, and raced up the road.

Nancy felt every sinew in her body stretch and contract as her legs pounded the freshly plowed blacktop. Her lungs felt as if they were on fire, about to burst. Ahead of them, Jean-Claude's carriage approached a bend in the road.

H-o-n-n-n-n-k! Instinctively Nancy jumped to the right. With a sickening squeal of tires, a black limousine swerved around her from behind, its horn blaring.

Neither she nor the Hardy brothers broke stride, except when their feet skidded. Ahead of them, the horse slowed down to take the bend.

"We're going to catch them!" Joe yelled.

But he had spoken too soon. The black limousine streaked past the carriage—and then screeched to a stop in front of it.

Its pathway blocked, the terrified horse shied and reared up on its hind legs.

"Hey!" shouted the driver, trying desperately to bring the horse under control.

Then the doors of the limousine opened.

"No!" Bess screamed.

Nancy watched in horror as three men in dark coats with revolvers burst out of the car.

White-faced, Jean-Claude and Bess climbed down from the carriage, their hands in the air.

"Stop!" Nancy shouted desperately.

121

Her cry was blown back by the chill wind. Not one of the men showed any sign of hearing her as Jean-Claude and Bess were roughly shoved into the backseat of the limo.

By the time Nancy and the Hardy brothers had reached the carriage, the limo was a hundred yards away, fishtailing on a patch of ice at top speed.

Chapter

Thirteen

"COME ON, FRANK! We've at least got to try to get the license number!" Joe yelled. He and Frank took off after the car, their feet skidding every so often. But the limo would be skidding, too, they knew.

Nancy's attention was caught by a moving figure off to her right—the carriage driver, stomping his way through the new-fallen snow off the road. She jumped over a snowbank and chased after him.

The snow on the lawn was deep and wet, and it clung to her shoes. The wintry air made her breath rasp in her throat after her jog to catch the carriage. It was almost impossible to summon any speed.

In seconds the man was at a low wall. He vaulted over without stopping.

He landed on the other side, facing Nancy for a second, and that was the first time she got a good look at his face.

It was the chestnut vendor. He stood frozen for a minute with the shock of being recognized.

"Look, we're on to you—we've got your name!" Nancy called out. "You might as well talk to me now!" It was a lie, but it might work—or at least stall him. She was only twenty yards from him and gaining.

The man's face was contorted into an angry snarl. "You tell your prince friend I'm gonna collect!" he shouted. Then he dropped down below the wall that separated them. When he came back up, he drew back his right hand and hurled something at Nancy's face.

Nancy lurched to the right as a ball of solid ice whooshed by her. She had landed facedown in the snow.

By the time she'd staggered to her feet, the man had disappeared into one of the side streets off the park.

Nancy brushed off the snow and trudged back toward the abandoned carriage. An image was etched in mind—the nightmarish sight of Bess shaking with fear as she was herded at gunpoint into the limo. If only I could have tried harder—run faster—*something!* Nancy thought. My friend's been kidnapped . . . Poor Bess—what's happening to you now?

Frank and Joe were back at the carriage when Nancy got there. "Find anything?" Joe asked.

Nancy nodded. "I sure did. The driver was our friend the chestnut vendor."

"*What?*" Frank said. "Why didn't Jean-Claude recognize him as soon as he got into the carriage?"

Nancy shrugged. "Who knows? Too wrapped up in Bess, I guess."

"So to speak," Joe muttered.

"The vendor said something strange— something about *collecting* from Jean-Claude," Nancy continued. "Maybe he wants Jean-Claude to pay him for the horse ride, but that doesn't explain much, does it?"

Frank scratched his chin in thought. "Maybe he means collecting on a bet. Maybe *that's* why these guys are after Jean-Claude."

"Could be," Nancy said. "How about you two? Did you get a plate number for the limo?"

"Too far away," Joe said. "Besides, it looked as though they'd covered it with mud."

"But we did find *this* on the road." Frank held up a small sheet of spiral-notebook paper. "It was right between the carriage and the limo. I can't make anything of it."

Nancy looked at it. In hastily scribbled pen marks was the notation $2340 / 2 = 117 + 22$. At the bottom was a circle with the number 139 inside.

"We don't know for sure that it means anything," Nancy commented. "Some third-grader might have dropped an assignment earlier."

"We thought of that, too," Joe said. "But it snowed outside for hours, and yet the paper is dry and the pen marks are almost completely legible. It couldn't have been out in the snow for more than a few seconds."

Nancy examined the paper again, perplexed. "They took two thousand three hundred and forty, crossed out the last digit, divided it by two, and added twenty-two. It must mean *something.*"

"Well, these guys don't work for free," Joe suggested. "Maybe they were figuring out how to split their fee."

"Great. Another fabulous lead." Nancy frowned and put the paper in her pocket. "What do we do now? Who knows where they'll take Bess?"

"Reynaud is bound to get a ransom note soon. That's when we might be able to pick up some clues," Joe said.

Nancy winced. How could Joe sound so calm about all this?

Frank gave Nancy a sympathetic look. "Joe's right. We'll notify Reynaud and then call the police. Meanwhile, we'll try to find Fiona and her father." Gently, he put his hand on Nancy's arm. "It's the best we can do."

Nancy just nodded. The lump in her throat made talking painful. Bess would be scared out of her mind, in the clutches of kidnappers who didn't care whether she lived or died.

Suddenly not much seemed to matter—the crown jewels, Jean-Claude, the burglars. As long as Bess was missing, Nancy knew she wouldn't be able to think about anything else.

Nancy, Frank, and Joe pushed through the revolving Winslow door. They darted across the lobby to the reservations desk.

A curly-haired man in a uniform looked up from his computer terminal. "Yes, may I help you?" he asked politely.

"We're looking for Dr. Fox," Nancy said. "Is he still a guest?"

The man punched a few keys on the terminal. "No," he said, shaking his head. "He checked out earlier today."

"Terrific!" Joe shouted in frustration, pounding the marble countertop.

The reservations clerk jumped back and gave Joe a hard look. "I'm sorry, sir," he said, "but it's not my fault."

"You're right. Sorry," Joe tossed back over his shoulder as he ran straight for the elevator, followed by Frank and Nancy. They pressed the button for Count Reynaud's floor.

"I'm not looking forward to telling our news to Reynaud," Joe said as the elevator ascended. "He's going to hit the ceiling. He's probably already having a fit about Jean-Claude. The way he shook off his bodyguards."

Nancy and Frank nodded. "Some bodyguards *we* are," Nancy said. "That's what he'll think, anyway."

They got off at the third floor and walked nervously toward Reynaud's suite. They could hear the muffled sound of his voice from all the way down the hall. As they got closer, the words became clearer.

"*Lexington,* you intellectual incompetent! You're on the wrong side of town!"

"I hate to interrupt an intimate conversation," Joe remarked. He squared his shoulders and rapped sharply on the door.

"Hang on!" Reynaud said. The door swung open. "Yes, what is—" Reynaud did a double take. "Come in. I was just on the phone."

They followed him in. When he returned to the phone, his voice had taken on a strained politeness. "Do you have that? That's right, Bloomingdale's is on *Lexington* Avenue. Yes . . . you're welcome. Goodbye."

He slammed down the phone and looked impatiently at the three detectives. "Well? How are Jean-Claude's new bodyguards? His old ones are *so* happy to have had the afternoon to do their holiday shopping." His voice was laced with sarcasm.

Suddenly Nancy felt very uncomfortable. "Not so well, I'm afraid," she said. "We, um— well, we seem to have lost him and Bess."

Reynaud's pen clattered to the desk. "You *lost*

him?" he repeated furiously. "How could you possibly— I suppose Santa Claus swooped down from the skies a few weeks early and took him away?"

"Well, no," Nancy replied. "Actually, it was a black limousine. And whoever it was took Bess, too."

Reynaud threw up his arms. "A black limousine. Wonderful!" He began pacing the room. "You realize the U.N. gala is tonight? Oh, this has gotten out of hand. Kindly walk out of this suite and never return—"

"Not so fast," Frank said. "We're in this too deeply to back out now. I'd suggest you think hard about your response to a ransom note, which I'm sure is on the way. I think the police will need to know—"

Reynaud's face suddenly went slack. "Police? Good heavens, they are the *last* people we should involve!"

"Count Reynaud," Nancy persisted, "the police will be a big help at this point. They have the staff and the know-how to deal with kidnappings."

"Never did I think *this* sort of thing would happen!" Reynaud stood up from his desk. "Your naïveté astounds me. Police involvement would result in instant press coverage—screaming banner headlines. I can just see it now. This event will become a circus, a disgrace to Jean-Claude, Sarconne, and myself." He pointed an accusing finger at Nancy. "I agreed to let you three help with protecting Jean-Claude, and look what has happened. I forbid the police—and I forbid any further involvement with you three. From now on, I and my staff shall handle this!"

Then he yanked his door open and said curtly, "Thank you for your visit. Good day."

"But—" Joe began.

"Come on, Joe," Frank said, taking Nancy's arm. "Let's go."

Nancy, Frank, and Joe went up to Nancy and Bess's room. "Have a seat," Nancy said in a dull voice. She was too upset to sit down herself. All she could do was pace.

"Reynaud is right about the publicity, you know," Joe said.

"Of course," Nancy replied, standing still for a second. "But what's more important? Bad publicity for Sarconne, or Bess's life? Sure, they won't harm Jean-Claude—but what if they use Bess as a bargaining chip? What if they threaten to kill *her* if the ransom isn't met? Count Reynaud wouldn't care!"

Just then there was a dull bumping noise at the door, as if something heavy had been pushed against it.

"What was that?" Nancy said. She began walking toward the door.

"Careful!" Frank warned. He and Joe jumped to their feet and stood behind her, ready for action.

A low, moaning sound came from the hallway. Cautiously Nancy turned the knob.

The door flew open—and into the room fell a body. Nancy gasped.

It was Jean-Claude!

Chapter

Fourteen

NANCY KNELT DOWN and tried to take in Jean-Claude's disheveled figure. His clothes were dirty and torn, his leather shoes scuffed and ripped, and his face covered with grime.

But his shoulders did begin heaving violently as she watched. Relief flooded through Nancy. He was alive!

"Are you all right?" Frank asked, kneeling down, too.

Jean-Claude nodded, his face flushed with exertion. "Out—out of breath—that's all. Please, may I come in?" He pushed himself to his knees.

"Of course." Frank helped Jean-Claude to his feet and led him in, followed by Nancy and Joe.

Jean-Claude slumped down onto Bess's bed. His hands were shaking. "They—they kidnapped me," he stammered. "They truly, truly kidnapped me!"

"And Bess? Where's Bess?" Nancy asked.

"I don't know! I—" Jean-Claude's voice wavered. He ran a shaky hand across his eyes.

Nancy sat next to Jean-Claude on the bed and patted his shoulder reassuringly. "Who are *they*, Jean-Claude? What happened?"

The prince gulped and pushed a lock of hair away from his forehead. "I don't know," he said. "Four men with masks, dressed in dark coats. I thought they might be—" He cut himself off. "I'd never seen them before. They took us to a building somewhere. They wanted to hurt me!"

"*Who* did you think they might be, Jean-Claude?" Nancy pressed.

Joe had been pacing up and down the room. Finally he wheeled around and stared furiously at Jean-Claude. "They kidnapped *you!* They wanted to hurt *you!* What about Bess, Jean-Claude? *Where's Bess?*"

Jean-Claude hung his head. "I—I really don't know. They were holding her in a different room."

"A different room *where?*" Joe continued.

"I couldn't tell. After they first took us, they blindfolded us and tied our hands. Then they seemed to drive around in circles. Two of them were having an argument in the front seat, but I couldn't hear what it was about. Finally one of them made a call on a phone in the car, and the next thing I knew, we were taken to some building, pushed up some stairs, and put in separate rooms. They gave me a chair to sit on and began tying my arms. They stopped when Bess's screaming became too loud in the other room."

"Screaming?" Nancy paled. "Were they— hurting her?"

"No, I don't think so. She was"—Jean-Claude's eyes misted over—"she was screaming my name over and over. The kidnappers were nervous about the noise, so they left to go to her room. That's when I realized my hands had been tied very well. I managed to untie myself and climb down a fire escape."

Nancy stared at him in disbelief. "And you just left Bess there—alone, screaming for help?"

"What could I do? There were at least three of them."

"So you ran away!" Joe said furiously. "They wouldn't have done anything to you, Jean-Claude. You're worth a lot to them alive. It's Bess they don't care about! It's *Bess* whose life means nothing to them! And just as I thought, it means nothing to you, either! You spoiled, worthless *coward!*"

Joe lunged for Jean-Claude, but Frank grabbed his arm from behind. "Stop it, Joe!" he snapped. "That's not going to help Bess!"

Jean-Claude had bowed his head sadly. He didn't even flinch at Joe's attack.

Joe looked as if he were boiling with rage. He wrenched himself away from Frank and stormed over to the other side of the room. He stood looking out the window, fists clenched, while Nancy turned to Jean-Claude. "Now, think hard," she said, fighting to stay calm. "When you left this building where they'd brought you, you must have caught the name of the street, right?"

"No," Jean-Claude said softly. "I was so afraid they were following me. I just ran and ran. It was a shabby place—old buildings, some of them totally abandoned. I thought I'd never get out, until I realized I was near an elevated train—"

"An elevated train? What stop was it?"

"Again, I don't know. But it was heading downtown, and after a while it went underground—and it let me off right behind the Winslow."

Nancy's face brightened a little. She dug a subway map out of her purse. "Okay, that narrows it down. Let's see—the only subway that stops here is the Lexington Avenue train, which goes down the East Side. Now, how many stops—"

Suddenly Nancy was interrupted by a booming voice from the doorway. "Young lady! Young lady, I must speak to you at once!"

Jean-Claude groaned. "Cousin Reynaud!" he muttered. "Oh, please, send him away!"

But Frank went to the door and opened it.

Count Reynaud burst in. His eyes were wide with disbelief and anger. *"Mon Dieu!* Jean-Claude, what are you doing here?" he exclaimed, in a strange, high-pitched shriek.

"Right this moment? I'm wishing you and your soothing voice were far, far away," Jean-Claude answered.

Count Reynaud stared at him for a moment, openmouthed. Then he walked up to Frank and faced him practically nose to nose. "I demand to know why you did not notify me *immediately* when you found Jean-Claude!"

"Well, Count Reynaud," Frank answered, "he just arrived a few moments ago, and, of course, we were about to—"

Reynaud turned away and walked right up to Jean-Claude. He shooed Nancy away with his hand and sat on the bed. "Oh, my dearest cousin," he said, "are you all right?"

"Couldn't be better," Jean-Claude said dryly. "I've just taken a marvelous new no-frills tour of Upper Manhattan. It's great fun—you wear a blindfold and listen to the tour guides get lost."

"Ever the jokester, even in times of stress," Reynaud said, his brow furrowed with concern. "I've been worried about you since our last— falling out. You have no idea how happy I am to see you well."

Jean-Claude smiled wryly. "Yes, I could tell by the joy in your voice when you first came in."

"Jean-Claude," the count said, "you should

know that your Cousin Reynaud always has your best interests at heart." He placed his hand on Jean-Claude's arm. "Now, why didn't you come to me first?"

Nancy glanced at Frank, who rolled his eyes. And from his corner of the room, Joe finally broke his silence. "Look, we're wasting time. I say we take Jean-Claude's limo and scour every block in whatever area he thinks Bess might be."

Reynaud looked shocked. "Don't be absurd! We can't just go traipsing around blindly in New York City—especially not the day of the U.N. gala. There are preparations, and—"

"I agree with Joe, Reynaud," Jean-Claude said. "You can stay if you like, but I intend to go with him."

"But—but I shall forbid the chauffeur—"

"You'll do nothing of the kind, Cousin Reynaud." Jean-Claude turned to the others. "Shall we?"

"Absolutely," said Frank. "But first we do have to call the police." The others nodded.

"I'll do that," Reynaud said. He went to the telephone, and as the others started to leave punched in 911.

As Nancy, Joe, Frank, and Jean-Claude headed out the main door of the hotel, Count Reynaud suddenly appeared. "Wait! I shall join you." Nancy caught a look that was almost worried on Reynaud's face. "I'm not much use here," he said. "I might as well keep an eye on my charge.

137

The police said they will keep their eyes out for Miss Marvin, but can't do much without more information."

After summoning the Sarconne limousine, Reynaud climbed in the front seat.

At a red light a few blocks later, François got into the left lane. "Shall I take the East Drive of Central Park?" he asked.

To their left, a block away, Nancy could see the edge of Central Park. Waiting by the curb were a half-dozen carriages and horses. "Good idea!" Nancy said. "But, first, maybe we can pick up some clues from those carriage drivers!"

"No!" Jean-Claude blurted out.

Nancy was startled by his strong reaction. "But they might know who—"

"No!" Jean-Claude repeated. "The carriage driver had nothing to do with it. It was the men in the limousine! We can't waste our time here!"

"But—" Nancy could hardly believe what she was hearing. What possible reason could there be for Jean-Claude to be acting this way?

"I suggest we start on the West Side," Reynaud cut in before she could press the matter. "It seems to me there are a lot of abandoned buildings there."

Jean-Claude laughed. "How would *you* know that?"

"Stay on the East Side," Joe said to the chauffeur. "That's where Jean-Claude picked up the subway after he escaped. We'll look around at each train entrance."

"Pardon me," François said. "Do you know the address?" He reached into his pocket to pull out a copy of a guide called the Manhattan Street Finder. "If you do, I can figure out the cross street. You see, there are wonderful little mathematical formulas here that help you—"

Suddenly Nancy had an idea. "We need to get to a newsstand," she said under her breath to Frank. Frank started to ask her why, but Nancy just nodded significantly at him.

Frank got the message. He stared at her blankly, but nodded slightly.

"I wish I *could* remember the address," Jean-Claude said. The limo sped past fancy shops and elegant brownstones, and the street numbers increased: Sixty-third Street, Sixty-fourth . . . Seventy-ninth . . . Ninety-sixth . . . After a while the neighborhood became more run-down. High-rise apartments alternated with rubble-strewn lots. And nothing looked familiar to Jean-Claude.

Just then Frank leaned over the front seat. "You get good mileage on this thing, François?" he asked.

"Terrible!" François replied. "This car eats a tank of gas in no time. Why do you ask?"

"Well, I was just noticing your gas gauge. I'd hate for us to run out here."

Nancy peered over the front seat. The gauge's needle was resting just above Empty.

"Good thinking," Reynaud said. "François, I

think our first order of business should be to find a station."

"But—but Bess—" Joe sputtered, but Nancy jabbed him in the side with her elbow, and he fell silent. "We passed a station just a few blocks ago," François said.

"Then turn around!" Reynaud said edgily.

François swung around a corner and drove back to the gas station. As they pulled up to the pump, Nancy glanced across the street. A group of shops—a laundromat, a market, and a candy and stationery store. "I think I'll get a snack while you're doing this," Nancy told François. "I'll be right back. Don't leave without me." She reached for the door handle with one hand and nudged Frank surreptitiously with the other.

"Joe and I will go with you," Frank said quickly.

The three of them walked across the street. As soon as they'd stepped inside the store, Nancy turned toward the counter.

"Do you have the Manhattan Street Finder?" she asked.

"Sure do!" the man behind the counter replied. He took down a laminated sheet from a rack behind him. "Three dollars."

"Hey, Nancy, don't buy that—François already has one that we can use," Joe objected.

Ignoring Joe, Nancy handed the man the money and then held out the sheet so that Frank and Joe could see it. "Take a good look at this thing," she said excitedly.

140

"What about it?" Joe asked.

"Don't you see?" Nancy said. "These are mathematical formulas to figure out where places are—just like the formula on this—" She reached into her pocket and took out the crumpled piece of paper she'd picked up in Central Park. Frank and Joe stared again at the cryptic figures.

$$2340 / 2 = 117 + 22 = 139$$

"The first number might be an address!" Frank said.

"Right," Nancy replied. She put the note and the address finder side by side on the table. "Now, it says here that you start with the number of the building, then cancel the last digit. Depending on what street the building's on, you add and divide by certain numbers to find out what cross street it's near."

"So we need to know on what street to divide by two and add twenty-two," Frank said.

The three of them pored over the list. And all at once, they saw it.

"Lexington Avenue," Nancy said. The building is at twenty-three-forty Lexington Avenue. According to this formula, that's at One hundred and Thirty-ninth Street."

Joe's eyes widened. "Let's go!" he shouted, reaching for the door.

"Wait!" Nancy warned. "Not so fast." She cast a quick glance out the window. Jean-Claude, Reynaud, and François were all still sitting in the car as the attendant pumped gas. "Did you guys notice anything funny about Jean-Claude's behavior on the way up here?"

Frank nodded. "He got all shook up when we suggested talking to the carriage drivers."

"That's right," Nancy said. "And that's not the only strange thing he's done the past couple of days."

"Really?" Joe said sarcastically. "I know plenty of people who climb buildings."

"Not that, Joe." Nancy's eyes darted from him to Frank. "Do you remember how Jean-Claude reacted after being kidnapped by the chestnut vendor?"

"Hardly fazed at all," Frank said.

"Right. And the same man just *happened* to be the driver of the carriage that kidnapped Jean-Claude. Why didn't Jean-Claude notice him? And why did the same man tell me that he was 'going to collect' from Jean-Claude? Could it be that he was also trying to 'collect' from Jean-Claude when he showed up at the Rockefeller Center rink?"

"Just a minute, Nancy," Frank said. "Are you saying—"

"You bet," Nancy said with fierce conviction. "Jean-Claude planned the whole thing. He had *himself* kidnapped!"

Chapter

Fifteen

FRANK AND JOE looked amazed.

"I don't know, Nancy," Frank said slowly. "If Jean-Claude masterminded all this, why would he have allowed his kidnappers to rough him up so badly at the club last night? He was incredibly upset afterward. Not to mention what he went through today."

"And how does Bess fit into all of this?" Joe said. "She said the muggers at the party went after her first—and when the two of them were taken today, the kidnappers went to *her* and left Jean-Claude alone!"

"I don't have the whole picture," Nancy said. "He might be lying, he might be a good actor—

he might even be innocent. But it's the only angle we have."

"True." Frank nodded. "But why would he do a thing like this in the first place?"

HONK! The sound of a car horn made them spin around. They looked outside to see that Jean-Claude's limo had pulled out of the station. Now it was waiting by the curb across the street.

"We're out of here," Joe said with a glint in his eye. "And I think we have a few questions to ask old Jean-Claude."

They walked outside. Immediately the rear door of the limo swung open and Jean-Claude waved them over.

"Come on," he said. "Reynaud was getting a bit impatient. He wanted us to go looking without you."

"Well, no need to do that, Count Reynaud," Frank said cheerfully. "Especially since one of the people in this car has known all along exactly where Bess is being held." He leaned forward and said, "Twenty-three-forty Lexington, please, François. That's at One hundred and Thirty-ninth Street."

Jean-Claude looked blankly at Frank. "What are you talking about?" he asked.

"How—where—?" Reynaud stammered. "This is an irresponsible accusation—"

"Is it?" Joe said accusingly, glaring at Jean-Claude. "I suppose it's not irresponsible to let yourself be kidnapped in broad daylight by a person whose face you should have recognized! A person you'd been making a deal with only an hour and a half before!"

"Wh-what?" Jean-Claude asked uncomfortably. Reynaud just stared at them, his mouth open.

Frank chuckled. "Oh, Joe's just flying off the handle. He got a little suspicious when we couldn't question the carriage drivers in front of Central Park. Imagine, he thinks that maybe you wanted to *keep* something from us!"

"Imagine," Jean-Claude said with a confused smile. "Well, that's all right, Frank. Joe does sometimes get a little hotheaded . . ."

"Hotheaded!" Joe bellowed. "It is hotheaded to be annoyed when someone's been lying to you since the first day you met him?"

"Wait a minute!" Jean-Claude said, sitting up defiantly.

"I think all Joe means is—well, it's funny, but it sure seemed as if you'd made some sort of *deal* with the chestnut vendor." Frank laughed. "Just *seemed.*"

Jean-Claude swallowed. He tried to laugh, but it came out sounding choked and unconvincing.

"Oh, by the way," Frank continued in a friendly voice, "I almost forgot. Your chestnut vendor friend left a message for you. He said he was going to collect!"

Joe's steel blue eyes were glinting with rage as he leaned toward Jean-Claude. "Yes, and we know exactly what the fee he was collecting was for, don't we?"

Nancy watched as Jean-Claude's face clouded over. He looked hunted, vulnerable. Now was the time for the finishing touch. Calmly she asked, "We want to know, Jean-Claude—why did you have yourself kidnapped?"

Count Reynaud looked as if he was about to explode. *"Stop the car at once!"* he yelled to François. "This has gotten completely out of—"

But Jean-Claude put his hand out to silence him. "No, go ahead, François. They're right. I did arrange it all."

For a moment the only sound was the humming of the limo's engine.

"Why, Jean-Claude?" Nancy said softly.

Jean-Claude looked around at the detectives' bewildered faces. From the front seat, Count Reynaud stared at him, stunned.

With a sigh, Jean-Claude slumped back in his seat. "I never meant to cause so much trouble," he said exhaustedly. "It's just that I've been feeling so *trapped.*" He stared listlessly out the window.

"In my country, everyone knows who I am. They shout at me in the streets, they throw me flowers and marriage proposals scribbled on notebook paper. Whenever anyone says my name, it's with respect and admiration. And when I wake up in the morning, I look out my window to a palace garden." He sat forward and looked from Nancy to Frank to Joe. He was frustrated.

"But you know what kind of dreams I always

seem to awake from? Dreams that I can walk into a movie, a restaurant, or down the street without a disguise, a chaperon, or bodyguard. I can just melt in with strangers and get to know them on their own terms.

"So whenever I get a chance to leave Sarconne, a whole world of possibility opens up. Many people in your country don't know me—people my own age, who like to do the things I like. People like you."

Jean-Claude cast a sheepish glance at Reynaud. "Unfortunately," he continued, "my cousin knows me all too well—and he watches me like a hawk. I know it's because he cares about me, but it only makes me want to break away." He shrugged. "And each time we travel together I have to think of a more elaborate scheme to do that."

"You had yourself kidnapped just to get away from Reynaud?" Nancy asked.

"I'm afraid so." Jean-Claude nodded. "I arranged a meeting with a man named Julius at a club the other night—the so-called chestnut vendor. For a thousand dollars he agreed to snatch me away from Reynaud in front of the Met—"

"I have *never* heard of such a thing," Reynaud said huffily. He folded his arms as if he'd been mortally insulted.

Jean-Claude didn't pay any attention. "By that time, I'd met Bess," he continued, his face reddening. "Not to mention you three. And we'd all had such fun that first night. Then, when you found out I was a prince, you still treated me as if I were a normal human being. I decided the best way to be around you was to convince Reynaud to let you be my bodyguards."

"In other words, you decided to use us," Joe snapped. "You figured we had nothing better to do!"

"I'm very sorry," Jean-Claude said. "Especially about"—he cast his eyes down—"about Bess. The more I saw of her, the more I found myself—well, I can't say here."

"Falling in love?" Nancy asked.

"Oh, *please!*" Reynaud said with a sneer.

Jean-Claude nodded without a word.

"How touching," Joe said bitingly. "And by this morning you were tired of us, too, and wanted to be alone with Bess."

"It seems so awful now, but I didn't mean any harm, I swear! Although I don't suppose my word means anything to you."

Jean-Claude fell silent a moment. Part of Nancy felt like reassuring him, but she also couldn't help feeling they had all been used.

"Anyway," Jean-Claude went on when no one said anything, "Julius met me at the rink, and we argued over a fee. Later he managed to bribe a carriage driver, and—"

"And you managed to blow it, anyway!" Joe exploded. "What happened, Jean-Claude? You didn't pay your friend Julius enough, so he decided to kidnap Bess until you paid him? Were you planning to sell the crown jewels tonight

148

because you were too cheap to dig into your own pocket—"

"No! No! Please!" Jean-Claude answered. "There is so much I don't understand! I had no idea who those men were at the club—and I didn't plan for the black limousine to overtake us! The men inside were strangers, I swear."

At that moment, François began slowing down. "Your building is to the left," he announced.

Startled, they all looked up. On that part of Lexington Avenue even the snow was grimy and dark from the soot falling from the elevated train tracks that ran above it. Old warehouses and abandoned factory buildings lined the street.

"Yes! Yes, that's it!" Jean-Claude exclaimed. "The old gray warehouse in the middle of that block to the left!"

"Stop here, François!" Nancy said. "We can't let them see a limo. We'll get out here. You wait with the limo on One hundred and Thirty-sixth Street."

"This is preposterous!" Count Reynaud sputtered. "I will not suffer the indignity of an—an American child making my chauffeur an accomplice to such nonsensical—"

"Do what she says, François," Jean-Claude ordered.

"Yes, sir," François said, turning right.

Nancy, Frank, Joe, and Jean-Claude got out of the limo onto the frigid winter street, leaving Reynaud smoldering inside. "If anything happens to me in this forsaken place, you'll be hearing from the consulate!" he warned as they shut the door and dashed toward the warehouse.

The warehouse stretched the entire length of the block. It was dingy and gray, and it looked as if it had been abandoned years ago. Paint chips clung to its sides, and many of the windows were boarded up. Above what had been the front door were rusted, rotting cast-iron numbers: 2340.

"This building is huge," Nancy said. "Frank, why don't you and I investigate the right side— Jean-Claude and Joe can take the left."

Nancy and Frank walked along the edge of the warehouse, stepping gingerly around huge plastic bags piled high against the wall. The snow had covered them, softening their edges until they were barely recognizable as garbage.

"What a terrible place," Nancy whispered, her breath coming out in white puffs. She moved closer to Frank, who turned to her with a confident, reassuring look. I'm glad he's here, Nancy thought, and once again she felt a prick of conscience. This was hardly the time to be thinking about Frank! Still, she couldn't help herself . . .

Nancy fought to focus her attention. Ahead of them, hugging the building, was a long object covered by a tattered old tarpaulin.

"What's that thing?" Frank asked.

"I don't know. Probably an abandoned car," Nancy replied.

Frank pulled up the tarp—and his eyes lit up. The gleaming hood of a late-model Cadillac limo reflected back at them in the fading wintry light.

"Bingo," Frank whispered.

Then a sudden bumping noise drew their attention upward.

Right behind the limo was a rusted emergency exit. A chain hung from the door handle, its lock open.

"Come on," Frank whispered, and they crept up to the door.

Nancy shivered. Suddenly she was keenly aware of the frigid wind whipping against her face. The howling of a dog drifted in from the distance. Slowly Frank pulled at the handle.

With a creak the door swung open, revealing a black void.

And out of the void came a pair of round steel muzzles, pointing directly at their faces.

Chapter
Sixteen

"THIS NEIGHBORHOOD really is frightening, isn't it?" Jean-Claude murmured as he and Joe walked around the left side of the building.

"Mm-hm," Joe answered absently, trying to ignore him. He was listening carefully for any noises in the snow-quiet street and watching for any sudden movements.

Clack! Joe and Jean-Claude spun as one to face a sound from across the street. A small man was rushing through the gate of a Cyclone fence behind another warehouse. The two boys ducked into a shadow to watch.

Painted on the side of the building were the words *Biltrite Factory Machinery,* and a fenced-in yard in back contained all sorts of tractors, forklifts, and backhoes. The man was wearing a Biltrite uniform. He slammed the gate, looked at his watch, and dashed away.

"Quitting time," Jean-Claude commented in a low voice.

Joe snorted. "He ought to be worried. He left the gate open." With that, Joe turned back to 2340 Lexington.

Jean-Claude continued to stare across the street at the yard full of vehicles. "You know," he said, "with the snow on them they look like a forgotten herd of dinosaurs, frozen in time. Don't they? The forklift like a Tyrannosaurus, the tractor like a Stegosaurus . . ."

Dinosaurs? Joe looked at Jean-Claude with disgust. He couldn't believe his ears. Here they were, trying to save the life of someone who was in danger because of Jean-Claude, and he was talking about dinosaurs! Patience, Joe, he said to himself. Nobody said this was going to be easy.

"Jean-Claude," Joe said as evenly as he could, "maybe you'd better—"

He was interrupted by a muffled scream and scuffling noises. "What was that?" he asked.

"It's coming from the other side of the building!" Jean-Claude answered.

Joe raced around to the front of the warehouse with Jean-Claude close behind. They sped past the boarded-up front door, past a broken window—

Joe pulled up short. Out of the corner of his eye

he had detected a movement inside the warehouse. He held his hand out behind him to signal Jean-Claude to stop. They crouched down and then raised their heads enough to look in through the window.

Framed in the jagged edges of the window's glass, two men in ski masks were forcing Nancy and Frank up a flight of stairs at gunpoint.

"Those are the men who kidnapped me!" Jean-Claude whispered. "The other two must be upstairs with Bess."

"We've got to get up there somehow," Joe muttered. He grabbed Jean-Claude by the arm. "Look," he said urgently, "one of us has to stay here and create some sort of diversion— something that will force all four of those goons out. The other will go up and try to free Bess, Frank, and Nancy."

"Right. Good idea," Jean-Claude said nervously.

For a second Joe hesitated. If he stayed downstairs, Jean-Claude would get the glory of rescuing everyone. But creating the diversion would be more dangerous. It would also take more skill. If it weren't done right . . .

Joe knew he had to do it. But before he could say anything, Jean-Claude said, "You go to the back of the building and wait. I'll create the diversion." He set his jaw. "I got us all into this, and I'll get us out."

Joe started to protest, but Jean-Claude cut him off. "I already know how I'm going to do it, Joe.

154

So I suggest you find a way to get to our friends right now."

"All right," Joe said reluctantly. "But you'd better not blow it."

Joe ran around to the back of the building. There, a dilapidated metal fire escape snaked down to the ground. It looked as if it were ready to collapse, but Joe knew it was probably his only way to get upstairs.

He perched underneath it and listened closely. From the second floor he could just hear the scraping of a chair, and some words from a soft, guttural voice:

"Put . . . in the same room . . . tie 'em . . . same mistake twice."

Joe heard nothing else. He glanced up. The window was just to the left of the fire escape. He'd be able to climb right into the room next to Bess's. All he had to do was wait for Jean-Claude's distraction—and hope it would work.

As he crouched stiffly in the cold, Joe felt as if hours were going by. Voices drifted out of the window and hung in the icy air.

A gruff, loud voice: "How did you find this place?"

Frank: "Well, wc came up Park, then took a right—"

Another tough voice: "Wise guy. Are you two alone?"

Nancy: "Our SWAT team is outside waiting for our signal."

A third unfamiliar voice: "I bet that prince showed you here, right? Where is he, huh?"

Crrrunnnnch! A loud, jarring, metallic noise stopped all conversation.

"What was that?" the first voice shouted.

Barrrrrooooom! This time Joe could feel the building shake. Now the tough voices sounded panicky.

"Someone's bombing the place!"

"I'll go down there—you guys keep watch!"

"No way! What if the place comes down? I'm not staying up here!"

"Me neither!"

"Me neither!"

Caaaaallllummmmp! This time no one stuck around long enough to say a word. Joe could hear frantic footsteps clattering down a metal stairway inside.

There was no time to waste. Joe climbed the fire escape ladder and waited on the second-floor landing. The metal platform creaked noisily, its iron supports beginning to come loose. Brick dust spewed out from where the supports were screwed into the wall.

A sheet of warped plywood had been placed over the glassless window. Joe reached up to pry it loose.

Just then another blast jolted the building. With a sickening metallic scrape, the iron supports slowly popped from the warehouse wall. The fire escape was falling to the ground, and Joe was along for the ride.

He still had his fingers wrapped around the plywood and prayed that it would support him as the fire escape collapsed in a tangled heap of clanging metal.

His fingers stiff with cold, Joe held tight to one edge of the plywood and swung his legs up until he could rest his toes against the ledge. Then the plywood started to give way, and Joe was leaning out from the building like a windsurfer steering his sail. Joe lunged at a single metal hook protruding from a brick. It held as the plywood flew to the ground.

Swinging his legs in, he found himself in a dark room with an old, lopsided wooden door at one end. Joe tried the door. It wouldn't budge.

He stepped back to charge it. This is going to make some noise, he thought, but I've got to take the chance.

Boom! Another rumble resounded through the building—and Joe took instant advantage. With a quick, sharp kick, he forced the door open. He stole out and found himself on a long balcony that gave him a view of the first floor.

Two men were gathered around the front door, frantically trying to secure it with pipes and metal debris, and the other two were blocking the fire escape door.

Joe darted into the first room next to him.

"Joe!" three voices cried. Frank, Nancy, and Bess—all tied to chairs—were staring at him.

Joe tried to smile. "Hey, you guys are missing all the action. Don't just sit there!"

He crouched behind Frank and untied him. Then together the two brothers freed Nancy and Bess.

Joe grabbed Bess's hand and ran out to the balcony after Frank and Nancy. "Take the stairs!" he called out. "The fire escape's history."

The four of them scrambled across the balcony to the metal staircase.

"Hey!" a voice called out from below them. "Where are you going?"

"Oh, no," Joe said. The masked men had seen them.

"You lousy punks," one of them growled. "Think you're so smart!"

He reached into his jacket and pulled out a revolver.

"Duck!" Joe yelled, yanking Bess to the floor as Frank and Nancy dove down. A shot rang out, followed by the sound of footsteps running toward them.

"What do we do now?" Nancy whispered. Joe looked around, thinking furiously. He couldn't let them down. *Where was Jean-Claude?*

Crrrrraaaaaaack! All four of them froze. It felt as if an earthquake had hit.

"He's—he's coming through!" a panicked voice screamed from below.

Joe, Frank, Nancy, and Bess jumped to their feet and looked over the balcony.

The four masked men were backing away in terror as the entire front door shook. Then, in an explosion of bricks and glass, the door fell in—

along with a large chunk of the wall surrounding it!

Joe felt his jaw go slack as his mouth fell open. Through a thick cloud of dust he made out a giant forklift—with Jean-Claude driving!

"Jean-Claude!" Bess screamed. She ran down the stairs.

"Bess, get back!" Joe shouted.

Below them, one of the four men fired his revolver at Jean-Claude.

"No!" Bess screamed.

"Come on! Let's get outta here!" one of the men yelled. The forklift barreled toward them, its Biltrite insignia vibrating with the motion. All four men dashed for the back door.

Bess was down the stairs and running toward the forklift. "Jean-Claude!" she kept calling.

Why wasn't he answering?

Then Joe caught a glimpse of Jean-Claude's face. It was covered with blood. And as Bess ran to him, waving her arms, he slumped forward, unconscious.

He must have been shot! Joe thought wildly.

The big machine suddenly leaped forward, picking up speed. Jean-Claude's foot had collapsed on the accelerator.

Joe's eyes widened with horror as he watched the mechanical monster head straight for Bess!

Chapter

Seventeen

Bᴇss ʟᴏᴏᴋᴇᴅ ᴀs ɪꜰ she wanted to run, but was glued to the spot.

The forklift was in high gear, only a few feet from her. It was narrowing the gap by the second.

Nancy and Joe, down the stairs now, ran toward her. "We're not going to make it!" Nancy gasped desperately.

But Frank had started for the forklift as soon as it came through the door. He was now up next to Jean-Claude and rudely shoved him aside. With a sharp yank of the steering wheel, he forced the forklift's tires to the left.

It swerved, its right wheels rising off the ground. Bess's shriek pierced the air.

And the huge, thick-treaded wheels passed by her with only inches to spare.

Nancy and Joe ran to Bess. Her entire body was shaking. "I—I was almost killed—" she whispered.

Joe put his arm around her and said, "You'll be all right. I'll take care of—"

Suddenly Bess snapped to. "Jean-Claude!" she blurted out. "Where's Jean-Claude? Is he all right?"

Frank was approaching them, Jean-Claude slumped at his side. "Get in!" he yelled.

Bess squeezed into the seat next to Jean-Claude. She put her hand on his chest, feeling for a heartbeat.

Nancy and Joe stepped up onto the foot ledges on either side of the cab and hung on tight as Frank drove the forklift back out through the massive hole in the wall and onto the street.

"He's breathing!" Bess exclaimed ecstatically.

"Yeah, he's going to be fine," Frank said. "Looks as though he was just scraped by some flying shards of glass."

"Ohhhh," came Jean-Claude's groggy voice. His head rolled from side to side for a moment. When his eyes opened, he abruptly pulled himself upright. "Bess! Wh-what happened? Did it work?"

"Yes!" Bess said, gazing into his eyes with an adoring smile. "You saved me, Jean-Claude! You saved us all!"

"The Tyrannosaurus came alive," Joe added with a chuckle.

Jean-Claude looked up. And for the first time since they'd met, he and Joe exchanged a smile.

The forklift chugged noisily down Lexington Avenue, bouncing up and down at each pothole. Nancy and Joe hung on tightly. "We're not taking this all the way to the Winslow, are we?" Joe asked.

"No, just to the next corner—One hundred and Thirty-sixth Street," Frank answered. "We'll go back in the limo."

At One hundred and Thirty-sixth Street, Frank pulled up. They looked left and right. There was no sign of the limo—or Reynaud. Frank blew the horn. No response.

"He's got to be here *somewhere*," Frank said. "We told him to wait."

"Look, I think we've spent enough time in this neighborhood," Nancy said. "Besides, the U.N. gala is in a couple of hours. If Reynaud's not here, I say we don't waste our time looking for him. Chances are he'll go back to the Winslow, anyway."

"Okay. Hang on," Frank said. He glanced up at the elevated train tracks. "We're going to find the nearest subway station."

By the time they reached One hundred and Twenty-fifth Street, Nancy felt as if her teeth were going to fall out from the cold and all the jarring from potholes. But finally they saw a set of stairs leading up to the tracks. The four of them clambered up just as a train pulled into the station.

After a few minutes the train plunged into an underground tunnel. From there it was only a few stops to the Winslow.

"We'd better take the back entrance," Nancy said as the group wearily climbed the subway steps. "We're a little beat-up-looking for the Winslow lobby."

At the hotel's back door, Nancy and Frank held open the door as Bess and Joe ushered Jean-Claude straight to the elevators.

"Let's take him to our room," Bess said. "We have some first-aid things there."

"Okay," Nancy replied. "Frank and I will meet you up there."

"Why? Where are we going?" asked Frank.

"We're going to look for Reynaud," answered Nancy. "I have a lot of questions to ask him."

Frank and Nancy got out of the elevator on the third floor. They walked over to Jean-Claude and Reynaud's suite and knocked on the door.

No answer.

"Count Reynaud, it's Frank Hardy and Nancy Drew!" Frank called out, knocking louder.

They waited again and knocked again—and again no one answered.

Finally Frank said, "Let's go back to your room and wait a half hour or so. I'll check downstairs to see if he's left us any messages. If he doesn't show up, we'll call the police."

They took the stairs up to the fourth floor. When they got to Nancy and Bess's room, Bess was dressing Jean-Claude's head wounds with alcohol and talking a mile a minute about the day's adventures. Joe was pacing grimly back and forth as he listened.

"So I told them, 'You can't keep me here! My friend Nancy will be after me in no time!'" Bess was saying. "Well, you should have heard them laugh. 'Nancy?' one of them said. 'Sounds like the name of a killer to me!' The *nerve* of them!"

Joe nodded tolerantly. "But what did they want, Bess?" he asked. "Did they say?"

"I wouldn't let them get a word in edgewise! I was so mad!" Bess replied proudly. "But I *did* hear them argue about something. One of them was saying they never should have taken Jean-Claude. The other one said something about its being too late now. For a second it almost seemed as if they were after *me,* not Jean-Claude!" She put away the alcohol and patted Jean-Claude on the head. "There! Good as new for the party tonight!"

Jean-Claude smiled and held her hand against his cheek for a second. "Thanks," he said. "I'll go get ready for the party. I'll see you all soon."

Joe shook his head after Jean-Claude had left. "It doesn't make any sense. Why would anyone want to kidnap *you?*"

Bess looked slightly offended. "Well, I—"

"Those muggers at the club last night—they

164

also went after you first," said Frank, who had stepped into the bedroom.

"That's right!" Bess said. "It is weird!"

"Very, very strange," Frank agreed. "It seems that of all of us, Bess would be the least important—" Bess gave him an outraged glare. "Sorry, Bess," he said with a laugh. "You know what I mean."

Joe cleared his throat. "Listen, we have to take this seriously," he said. "What if they *are* after Bess? Could it be she has something they need?"

"Of course not—" Bess began.

"Think, Bess," Joe continued. "Have you bought anything valuable lately? Has Jean-Claude given you anything that those men might want? I know it's a long shot, but—"

Bess shook her head, bewildered. "Joe, the only things I have here are my clothes, my makeup, some magazines, and a few Christmas gifts I bought—you know, perfume, chocolates, clothing. I mean, it's nice stuff—but not nice enough for someone to kidnap me!"

Joe nodded and turned away. "Yeah. I'm sorry, Bess. I'm just grasping at straws."

"Speaking of those gifts," Bess said with a glint in her eye. "I am absolutely *starved*. In one of my shopping bags there's an absolutely irresistible chocolate crown—it wouldn't surprise me if the kidnappers were after that. Joe, what did you do with all my stuff?"

Joe pointed into a corner of Bess's room. Boxes

and bags in red, green, gold, and silver were stacked so high they looked like an insecure Christmas tree. "Uh, I know it's hard to tell, but I brought the bag in here yesterday."

Sure enough, stuck in the back was a silver bag that said Chocolate Revelations. Bess scampered over and brought it to the bed. "Wait till you see this," she said, lifting the wooden box out of the bag. "Not only is it gorgeous, but it's *solid* chocolate!"

Bess opened the box and took out the chocolate crown.

"Hey, I've seen one of those before," Joe said, staring at the crown. "Now, where was it?"

"Sorry, the guy told me it was a one-of-a-kind design," Bess said. She lifted the crown and took a big bite.

"Yechhh!" she said, spitting the chocolate out. "That is the weirdest filling! It tastes like *plastic!*"

"Hey, let's see!" Frank picked up the chocolate and examined it. A yellow, claylike filling oozed out onto his hand.

"It is plastic, all right," he said, his eyes flashing with recognition. "Plastic explosive!"

Chapter

Eighteen

Ugh!" Bess cried out. She ran to the bathroom to wash out her mouth.

Frank quickly broke open the crown. Sure enough, it had only a thin layer of chocolate. Inside was a light, crown-shaped container covered with the yellowish substance.

"Plastique," Frank said. "I've seen this stuff before. The terrorists' dream, they call it. You smear it over some sort of detonator—" He held up the plastic-coated object. "Which is probably what we have here. Then it's set off by radio signals—usually two of them, in sequence."

"So the kidnappers *were* after Bess," Nancy said. "They wanted the bomb!"

Frank nodded. "Which means that either Jean-Claude was double-crossed by the kidnappers he hired, or—"

"Or he didn't hire them at all!" Joe interrupted. "That must be it! Remember what he said in the limo? He had no idea who those guys in Central Park were."

"Exactly," Frank replied. "We're dealing with a second set of kidnappers—*real* kidnappers."

"But why didn't they ever ask me where the crown was," Bess wanted to know. "I'd have told them."

"Maybe they were waiting for their boss to come and question you," Frank said.

Nancy nodded slowly to herself. It was all becoming clear now. "They were the ones who dropped the piece of paper with the address. It probably happened in the scuffle."

"So they got angry and dumped Jean-Claude in the car, even though they didn't need him," Frank conjectured. "And once they got to the warehouse, they started thinking they should have left him behind."

"That explains the arguments Bess heard," Joe said.

"And the break-ins," Nancy added. "First they tried our suite and didn't find anything. Fortunately, Bess's bag was in your room then. Then the next night they broke into Frank and Joe's suite—"

Joe shook his head. "But how could they have made the connection?"

"Because they had seen us at the club earlier that night," Nancy said. "Where we had to fight them off Bess!"

"That's right," Frank said. "And they only started fighting Jean-Claude when he interfered."

Joe laughed. "They must have been furious when they tried our suite and found the bag wasn't there, either! I had brought it back to Bess's."

By now Bess had come back into the room and was staring, crestfallen, at the ruined crown. "This is awful. I should never have talked that guy at the chocolate shop into giving me this thing. I—I should have let him send it away the way he was supposed to."

Nancy, Frank, and Joe all looked at her. "Send it away?" Frank said.

"Yes. It was some kind of special shipment, the guy said." Bess took a step back. "D-don't all look at me like that. They—they just looked so good, all sitting there on that metal tray—"

"They?" Joe said. "How many were there?"

"I don't know! Twenty, maybe—"

"*Think,* Bess—this is important!" Nancy said. "Where were they being sent? Did he say?"

Bess nervously pulled a strand of hair behind her ear. "N-no, he didn't—"

"We've got to find out!" Joe said firmly. "Can you show us where the shop is, Bess?"

"Sure. It's just down the block from—"

Bess was interrupted by a sharp rapping on the door. Joe sprang up to answer. "Yes?" he said.

"Reynaud," came the voice outside.

Joe pulled the door open. "Count Reynaud! Where were you?"

Count Reynaud nodded gravely as he walked in. "I must apologize, my young friends. I'm only happy that you all were able to return safely from that wasteland."

"What happened, sir?" Nancy asked.

Reynaud looked gray and tired, as if he'd just been through an ordeal. "You see, François and I parked on that terrible, abandoned street. Soon we saw a rather rough group heading toward the car, and—"

"Uh, excuse me, Count Reynaud," Joe interrupted. He looked back at the others. "I'm going to head over to Chocolate Revelations now. It shouldn't take too long—*if* they're still open."

"Wait!" Bess said. She got up and ran to his side. "I'm going with you! I've done nothing but mess things up so far. The least I can do is help you out."

Nancy smiled. "Okay," she said. "Frank and I will meet you there in a few minutes."

"We'd have been better off if we walked," Joe muttered to Bess. Their cab was inching along Fifty-seventh Street in the late rush-hour traffic. All around them, Christmas lights lit up the night sky, and the sound of bells mixed with the blare of angry horns.

"There it is!" Bess exclaimed. "Right near that vendor!"

Joe looked over to the sidewalk. There, a woman in a threadbare coat sat patiently on a stool by the curb, tending to a cart full of candies and nuts in glass jars. Just to her left was the chocolate shop.

The cabdriver pulled over to the curb, took a deep sniff, and smiled. "No wonder you were in such a hurry to get here," he said. He turned around and winked. "Now, don't eat too much of that stuff—it'll kill you!"

Joe reached up to pay him as Bess got out of the cab. "You don't know how right you are," he said.

The overpowering aroma of chocolate greeted Joe as he climbed out. He glanced up and immediately saw where it was coming from—a window that was open a crack on the second floor.

"Oh, no!" Bess cried out. "We're too late!"

Joe looked down to see her staring at a sign on the front door:

Making Delivery
Be Back Soon

"Great," Joe answered. "We've got to get in there—somehow."

Bess grimaced. "Please don't say we have to break through the door. It's glass!"

Joe looked at the door and the large plate-glass window. Thin silver tapes ran along the edges of both. Each tape was attached to a little sensor by wires.

"No," he said. "We'd set off an alarm. There's got to be another way . . ."

He caught another whiff of chocolate and looked up again. A smile crossed his face as he saw small wisps of steam floating out of the second-floor window.

"Oh, no you don't!" Bess said, seeing the glint in his eye. "Are you crazy? You can't climb up there with all these people walking by! Someone will see you."

Joe didn't have to look around to know Bess was right. He could feel the crowds of Christmas shoppers jostling him on either side as they spilled out of buildings and into subway entrances. With an agitated sigh, he said, "Look, Bess. There's no alleyway, no one inside, nothing. Now we could sit around and wait till someone comes back. That way we definitely could find out where the bombs were delivered. We'd just have to follow the sound of the explosion." He gave Bess a level gaze. "Somehow I don't think that's the best solution, do you?"

"No, but these people . . ." Bess glanced around nervously. "I mean, they're not all going to just walk by and ignore you!"

"Well, they *might*," Joe said, slowly raising an eyebrow, "if they have something to distract them . . ."

Bess began shaking her head in disbelief. "You mean—you don't expect *me* to—wh-what am I supposed to do?"

"I don't know. Make some sort of commotion."

"What kind of commotion? I'm not good at this kind of thing, Joe!"

"You'll figure something out." With that, Joe turned toward the building. "But do it fast."

"But—"

"Please, Bess!"

Bess looked nervously around as people pushed by her. "Sure—sure, Joe," she mumbled.

Joe examined the brick facade of the building. A cast-iron Chocolate Revelations sign stuck out just above the first-floor window. There were filigrees in the sign that he could grab onto and hoist himself up. From there it would be a short reach to the ledge of the second-floor window.

"I've had that urge myself!" came a voice behind Joe. He spun around to see a young woman wearing a pin-striped business outfit and sneakers. She smiled at him and disappeared down the subway steps.

Joe sighed. Perfect, he said to himself. *Everyone* is going to notice this. He looked back at Bess, who seemed to be wandering aimlessly on the sidewalk. Come *on*, Bess! he wanted to yell out to her.

Just then, as if she had heard his thoughts, Bess turned around. But instead of looking at Joe, she walked slowly, lazily backward along the curb.

She's chickening out, Joe thought. I *knew* it. We're sunk! He rolled his eyes and looked back at the building.

"Hey—*hey!*" a shrill voice called out. "Watch where you're—"

Crash! Joe's eyes popped open as a sea of peanuts, cashews, chocolate-covered raisins, and hard candy cascaded onto the sidewalk.

In the middle of it all, sprawled out on the sidewalk next to the toppled cart, was Bess.

"You clumsy little fool!" the sidewalk vendor screamed at Bess. "Look what you've done! Do you have any idea how expensive this stuff is?"

Instantly a crowd gathered around Bess. Two men reached down to help her up.

"Oh, I'm so sorry!" Bess said, looking flustered and embarrassed. "I—I must have been looking backward . . ." She pulled a pad and pencil out of her shoulder bag. "Here, let me give you my father's name and number. He'll pay for everything."

Joe smiled to himself as the throng of people grew. Within seconds, it seemed that everyone on the block was coming over to see what had happened.

Wasting no time, he looked both ways—and jumped. His right hand clutched onto one of the sign's filigrees. Digging his toes between two bricks, he pulled himself up. Then he grabbed onto the ledge of the open window and boosted himself into the building. With a self-satisfied grin he thought to himself, She thinks Jean-Claude is the *only* guy who can climb buildings, huh?

Stepping into the room, he looked around in awe. In the center was an enormous steel vat, attached to about twelve different gauges—and filled with bubbling, molten chocolate! On a far table there were steel chocolate-bar molds along with temperature-recording devices and a computer screen.

Joe ran back over to the window. Below him, the crowd was beginning to break up. A nearby shopkeeper was sweeping up the debris with a push-broom. Backing up toward Chocolate Revelations, Bess was thanking the men who had helped her.

Joe sped downstairs and opened the front door. "Come on, you've got to see this place!" he said. "It's pig heaven!"

Bess was beaming. "I did it, Joe!" she exclaimed. "Did you see me out there? Not bad, huh?"

"Oscar material," Joe said. "I'm glad I won't be around to see your father's reaction when he gets the bill." He ushered Bess into the front door and up the stairs.

Bess's face was rapturous as she took in the sight and smell of the second floor. She looked over the edge of the vat. "I feel like diving in," she said.

"I wouldn't," Joe said, punching some keys on the computer. "The flies'll chase you home. Okay—let's see what we can find here."

Just then a menu popped on the screen:

ACCOUNTS PAYABLE
ACCOUNTS RECEIVABLE
DELIVERY ORDERS
EMPLOYEE RECORDS
PAYROLL

"Let's start with Delivery Orders. If we can find out where they're planning to send these things, maybe we can figure out what they're for." Joe moved the cursor to Delivery Orders and scrolled down to December.

"Did you find anything?" Bess asked, looking over his shoulder.

"Yep. Here it is!" Joe said. Together they stared at the words on the screen:

SPECIAL SHIPMENT

DATE: DECEMBER 21
NUMBER OF BOXES: 4
ITEMS PER BOX: 5

DESCRIPTION: CHOCOLATE REPLICAS, 15TH
CENTURY CROWN—REIGN OF KING ANTONIN,
SARCONNE (ON EXHIBIT AT MET)

DESTINATION: UNITED NATIONS, C/O SARCONNE
CONSULATE, PENTACENTENNIAL GALA

DELIVERED: YES

Bess gasped, and Joe felt the blood draining from his face. He thought back to the jewel-

176

studded gold crown at the Met—the crown that he had only glanced at casually. "I knew that chocolate thing looked familiar!" he exclaimed.

"We've got to get over there, Joe!" Bess said, grabbing him by the sleeve. "There are twenty of them—twenty bombs set to go off at Jean-Claude's party!"

"Nineteen," Joe answered with dread, pushing his chair back. Together they ran to the door.

A sudden, piercing whistle made Joe stop short before they got there.

"Come *on!*" Bess cried out. "What are you doing?"

"That's Frank's signal," Joe said. "It means danger." He ran to the window and leaned out to look down at the street.

Instantly he tensed. Two familiar-looking men were breaking the front door down—two of the thugs from the warehouse!

"Careful, Joe!" came Frank's voice over the scream of the alarm as the men made it through the door. Joe watched his brother and Nancy jump out of Jean-Claude's limo at the curb. Frank gestured to the door. "There are four of—"

"No!" Bess's scream pierced the air. "Get your hands off me!"

Joe spun around. One of the men had grabbed Bess by the arm. Another man was thundering up the stairs behind him. "Leave her alone!" Joe shouted. He rushed over and yanked Bess's attacker back by the collar.

The man wrenched loose and faced Joe head on. "Just try to stop me, kid!" he snarled.

"No problem," Joe answered, drawing back his fist. The man stood firm, a smug grin showing through the opening in his ski mask.

Joe put all his weight behind his thrust—and found himself suddenly jerking backward. Another one of the thugs had grabbed his neck from behind. With all his strength, Joe tried to pry the man's arm away.

"Let's sweeten his disposition a little," the first one grunted—and let loose with a punch to Joe's abdomen. Bess screamed at exactly the same pitch as the wailing siren.

For a moment, everything went black. Joe's body slumped.

But when his eyes opened, he was flying through the air—toward a deep, hot, churning mass of molten chocolate!

Chapter

Nineteen

JOE PLUNGED INTO the vat of thick, gooey liquid. The temperature wasn't unbearable. He struggled to his knees and tried to open his eyes, but they were weighted down by the sticky heaviness of the chocolate. Before he could raise his hand to his face, he felt a viselike grip on his shoulders.

"Try some more," the guttural voice said, pushing Joe down. "It's good!"

Joe disappeared under the chocolate. He struggled desperately against the unseen hand, but it was as if he were in quicksand. His lungs hurt agonizingly. This is it, he thought—the first person in history to drown in a vat of chocolate!

Then a strange, hollow sound made its way through the chocolate to Joe's ears. And at the same time, the grip on his shoulder loosened.

Joe propelled himself to the surface. Instinctively he sucked in a mouthful of air, taking in about a quarter-pound of chocolate with it. Coughing violently, he wiped away the chocolate from his eyes and saw Nancy standing over the inert figure of the masked man. Over her head she held a shiny steel chocolate mold.

"Look out!" Joe shouted. Behind Nancy, another masked man rushed up holding a length of clear tubing between his two hands.

Nancy spun around and stepped aside. As the man charged past her, she grabbed the tubing and pulled. The man somersaulted across the floor.

Joe grabbed the side of the vat and pushed down, trying to boost himself up and over. Suddenly he felt the vat tipping forward. It wasn't going to support his weight! His hand slipped, and he plunged back inside.

When Joe came back to the surface, he was facing the other side of the room, away from the door. The computer was still lit up with the delivery information. In front of it, Frank was facing the other two masked men in a karate stance.

"Okay, fellas," he said through gritted teeth. "You remember how much fun this was at the club." He lunged for them. But he stopped short as they each pulled a gun.

"Run!" Frank yelled to Nancy and Bess. The girls backed off toward the door. The men pulled up their masks, and Frank saw their faces for the first time. One had dark, hawklike features, and the other was bald and pasty-skinned. They swung from Frank to the girls, not knowing where to shoot.

Joe braced his left foot on the rim of the vat. With a mighty heave, he lifted himself out of the chocolate. The other end of the vat flew upward, sending Joe plunging toward the floor and shooting an arc of chocolate.

"Let's go!" Joe yelled, sliding toward the door and pulling the chocolate down off his face and hair.

Frank shoved his two attackers into the rushing flood of molten chocolate. Then he ran to the door just behind Bess and Nancy.

Slipping and tumbling, covered with chocolate, Joe reached the exit. He could hear confused grunts and shouts behind him as he slammed the door and sprinted downstairs, where the alarm was still wailing. Still no police. Bursting out the front, he ran to the open door of the limo, leaving chocolate footprints in the snow.

"When it dries, we'll break it off and eat it!" Frank said.

Joe climbed in and made a squishing sound as he hunkered in the backseat.

Nancy gave him a deadpan look. "You look awful, but you smell great!" she said.

But Joe was in no mood to joke. He wiped

away some of the chocolate from his arms and legs and rubbed the crystal on his watch so he could look at it. "The U.N., François," he said. "And *fly!*"

The automatic door locks clicked into place as François pulled the limo smoothly away from the curb.

Joe turned to Frank and Nancy. "We saw the shop's delivery schedule," he said grimly. "The chocolate bombs were sent to the Sarconne party at the U.N.!"

Frank groaned. "Of course! They're miniature replicas of the Sarconne crown! Why didn't we recognize them?"

"Let's just hope we're not too late!" Nancy said.

Then Joe wiped more chocolate off his face and looked around. "Hey, what happened to the two gentlemen from Sarconne?" he asked.

"Reynaud wouldn't let Jean-Claude come," Frank said. "He had to get ready for the gala. But he insisted Nancy and I take the limo. According to him, François is the best driver in the business." He glanced at François. The driver was concentrating intensely as he swerved around a line of cars and through a yellow light—just before it turned red. "I guess Reynaud is a good judge of some things," Frank added.

François gave a tight little smile and kept his eyes on the road.

Bess was staring out the window, her face

twisted with anxiety and fear. "Oh, the delivery man's probably already *there,*" she moaned. "Can't we go faster?"

"I just do what I'm told, ma'am," François said.

That seemed like a strange answer, but Joe was too tired to question it. Instead, he put a sticky arm around Bess. "It's okay," he said. "It's seven o'clock now. Reynaud and Jean-Claude are just getting there. Dinner isn't until eight, and it won't be until dessert that . . ." Joe trailed off as he realized he'd just smeared chocolate on the back of Bess's dress.

Bess wheeled to face him. "That Jean-Claude is blown up! Is that what you're trying to say?" Tears were forming in the corners of her eyes. "Some crazy terrorist is going to kill Jean-Claude, and you're telling me it's okay?"

Nancy leaned over to Bess. "Joe's just trying to tell you that we'll make it in time," she said comfortingly. She sighed and looked out the window with Bess. "Where are we?" she asked François.

"A shortcut, miss," he replied.

Then she turned back to Bess and the brothers. "What I can't figure out is *why* this is happening. I mean, they had a million chances to kill Jean-Claude!"

"Maybe they want the publicity," Frank said.

"If they wanted publicity, they could have gotten him at Rockefeller Center, the rock club,

Central Park—all crowded places." Nancy turned to Frank and Joe. "They're using explosives that could wipe out the entire Sarconne delegation, plus who knows how many more in the U.N. building. It's extreme. Somehow it doesn't seem worth it."

Bess, curious now, was straining to look at the street signs. She tried to open the window, but the button wasn't working. "Why aren't we there yet? Where's the U.N. building?" she fretted.

François was silent.

Frank looked at him quizzically. He, Nancy, and Joe all stretched forward to peer through the windshield. Above them passed a big green sign that said: West Side Highway and Piers. Ahead of them stretched a crumbling overhead highway. On either side were grimy old industrial buildings.

"This doesn't seem right," Joe said.

"You'd better believe it doesn't," Nancy added. "The U.N. building is on the *East* Side, not the West! François, where are you taking us?"

Without a word François reached under the dashboard and flicked a switch. A thick Plexiglas barrier shot up from the back of his seat toward the ceiling, cutting him off completely from his four passengers.

"François! No!" Nancy cried. All four of them tried to pull the barrier down, but the motor was too strong. They had to slip their hands away at the last minute.

"You can't do this!" Bess shrieked, banging frantically on the barrier.

"This is an emergency, François!" Frank pleaded.

"I just do what I'm told, sir," François repeated, his eyes never leaving the road. And the limo sped farther and farther away from the U.N.

Chapter

Twenty

NANCY TRIED THE door handle. She pressed the window button. Frank pounded on the Plexiglas barrier, and Joe tried to kick the door open. Nothing worked.

"We're trapped!" Bess said. "This is like—like a moving prison!"

Then Frank slammed his fist into the palm of his other hand. "Reynaud!" he said. "How stupid could we have been! It was Reynaud all along! *Reynaud* knew our room numbers, and he was with us at the club—it was a piece of cake for him to arrange the break-ins and the mugging."

"Of course! And he must have had Jean-

Claude tailed through Central Park this morning," Joe said.

Nancy shook her head in frustration. "And that phone conversation we overheard—he was shouting 'Lexington Avenue' to someone. No wonder he insisted on going with us to find Bess, and then wanted us to drive up the West Side. He *wanted* François to take us around in circles!"

"But why?" Joe asked. "I know Jean-Claude and Reynaud aren't crazy about each other, but what possible reason would Reynaud have to—"

"Stop!" Bess blurted tearfully. "What's the difference? I mean, here we are about to be dumped into the river—or maybe old François will spare us if we give him the bomb so he can murder Jean-Claude—and all you can talk about is *why, why, why!*"

Nancy looked into Bess's eyes. She'd never seen her friend so torn apart. Should I give him the bomb? Nancy asked herself. Instinctively her hand felt her shoulder bag. The bomb was still there.

Then Nancy realized that giving François the bomb wouldn't help anything. The terrorists wouldn't need it—they had nineteen other bombs already. And François probably knew that.

Frank and Joe were looking around, thinking of ways to escape. Bess was staring hopelessly at Nancy as if waiting for her to make a move. François was now driving around a police barricade, steering the limo up an abandoned, snow-covered ramp.

Somehow Nancy had the feeling François wasn't going to let them off easily. If only there were some way she could get through to him . . .

Suddenly she knew exactly what she had to do. She reached into her bag.

And she saw all three of her friends' eyes widen as she dug out a familiar yellow claylike substance.

"No, Nancy," Bess said under her breath. "You wouldn't!"

Nancy gave Bess a sharp look. In a voice loud enough for François to hear, she said, "We have no choice, Bess."

With a broad motion, she smeared the stuff on François's Plexiglass barrier. "Recognize this, François?" she said.

François blanched, and an uncertain grin twitched on his face. "Young lady, do you have any idea what you're playing with?" he asked.

"I don't know. Maybe you can give me some advice." Nancy shoved her hand back into her bag, ripped the detonator out of the chocolate bomb, and planted it firmly in the gooey mess on the barrier. "Is this right so far?"

The limo screeched to a stop. When François spun around, his jaw was quivering. "Now, see here—"

"No, *you* see here!" Nancy retorted. She reached into her bag once again, pulled out her portable radio, and took the cover off the battery housing. Then she tore out the wires from her headphones. Holding them up close to the detonator, with the batteries in her other hand, she looked straight into François terrified face.

"If we're going to go, François," she said simply, "you're going with us." With that, she plugged the headphones into the radio and turned it on.

François hit the lock release. All the locks popped open. Shaking wildly, François pushed his door open and fell out. He scrambled to his feet, and—without looking back—he ran down the ramp, holding his ears and screaming.

At last Nancy dropped the wires. "Let's get out of here!" she said.

She and Frank opened the doors and sprang out. But as soon as Nancy put one foot on the road, her body stiffened. She had just seen what was coming.

Near the base of the ramp, another limo was racing toward them. Four men with sunglasses were inside. All but the driver were hanging out the window with guns drawn.

"Uh-oh. It's the return of the chocolate soldiers," Frank said. He jumped into the driver's seat as Nancy fell in the back. "Hang on!" Frank said—and floored the gas pedal. With a screech of tires, the limo tore off, swerving on the frozen crust.

Nancy, Bess, and Joe crouched low in the seat.

Joe quickly popped his head up to look out the back window. "Piece of cake," he said happily. "They're having more trouble than we are."

A shot rang out from behind them. The limo went faster, despite the fact that it was still fishtailing and climbing up the ramp—and up—and up . . .

Suddenly Nancy and Bess and Joe were thrown violently against the front seat. Frank had hit the brakes—flat to the floor. The limo swerved left and right and around in a full circle before grinding to a full stop.

"Hey, what's going on?" Joe shouted.

"Get out!" Frank ordered.

Joe gestured toward the other limo. "But—"

"Do it! And stay low."

Frank and the others pushed their doors open, slithered along through the snow—and pulled up short.

Nancy's heart sank. They were all lying flat, looking down thirty feet over the edge of the road. The road had obviously collapsed years earlier. If the limo hadn't stopped when it did, they would have flown off and dropped onto the crowded highway below.

"No wonder this ramp was blocked off!" Joe said. Most of the chocolate had rubbed off his coat.

There was a crash and what sounded like a gunshot. Quickly Nancy looked over her shoulder. She had been half right—it was a crash and a blown tire! The other limo had run into a large piece of metal that had been hidden in the snow.

"Quick. Follow me!" Frank called. He went to the extreme left edge of the road and started to clamber hand over hand down a rusted steel beam.

Nancy followed him and, when she was at the bottom, looked back up. Frank was successfully stopping the traffic.

Bess was standing there shaking and clutching Joe's arm, her face dead white.

"Come down!" Nancy shouted.

"I can't!" Bess whimpered. "I'm afraid of heights!"

Another shot rang out.

"I lied," Bess said. Quickly she sat down at the edge of the road and began scrambling down.

"Hurry!" Joe yelled. Clutching onto a crossbeam, he lowered himself after Bess.

Nancy started across the street. But a sharp cry from Joe made her spin around.

She turned to see one of his hands slip from the beam. As he dangled with his other hand, Nancy spotted a gunman leaning over the side of the road, taking aim at Joe.

"Jump, Joe!" she yelled.

Joe let go and fell to the ground, rolling out into a sprint. With a burst of speed, they all darted across the traffic and onto a side street.

They ran to the end of the block. An unoccupied taxicab was just pulling away from a gas station when they got there. "Stop!" Nancy shouted.

The driver skidded to a halt, and all four crowded into the backseat. "The U.N.!" Frank panted. "It's an emergency!"

"Gotcha!" the driver said as he floored the accelerator.

The four of them huddled together in the seat, warming up and gasping in lungfuls of air, depleted from their frosty run.

"Whew. That was close," Nancy said.

"*Close?*" Joe said with disbelief. "I thought you were going to blow us to bits! How—how could you be so reckless with the plastique?"

Nancy smiled. "What plastique?"

She looked over to see three pairs of dumbfounded eyes.

"Oh, the stuff on the Plexiglas!" she said with a mischievous smile. She reached into her bag and pulled out a small plastic tub. On it were the words *La Boue de Visage: European Facial Regeneration Treatment.*

Bess's face broke out into a broad smile. "The face mud from Bloomingdale's!" she crowed. "I *told* you that stuff would come in handy!"

"Face mud!" Joe groaned, rolling his eyes. "I thought you'd lost your mind!"

"Mmmm-*mmmm!*" came the cabdriver's voice. His smiling eyes were staring at them in the rearview mirror. "One of you eating a chocolate bar or something?" he asked.

Joe slumped back self-consciously in the seat. "Just keep driving," he mumbled.

In a few more minutes they were at the U.N. They raced around to the main entrance, where a receptionist sat at a high marble desk. Behind her, in white letters on a black felt board, was a sign that said "Sarconne Pentacentennial— Room 610."

"Sarconne gala, please," Nancy said.

"Elevators are to your right," the receptionist answered, without looking up from her work. "See the security guard on the sixth floor for clearance."

They ran to the elevator and got off at the sixth floor. The sound of Christmas carols filled the hallway as they approached an elaborate security setup. A metal detector arched across the hall, and four armed guards were watching them approach.

Nancy put on the most composed-looking smile she could. But it didn't keep the guards from noticing Joe.

"What'd you do?" one of the guards called out to him. "Roll in the mud?"

"It's chocolate," Joe said matter-of-factly, peeling off a piece from his sleeve. "Want some?"

The guard gave him a drop-dead stare.

Quickly Nancy said to another guard, "Uh— Drew, Hardy, Marvin. We should be on the list."

The second guard frowned and looked down the list. "Drew . . . Hardy . . . Marvin . . ." he muttered.

"Hold it, Ralph!" the first guard said. She leaned over the desk, the supervisor tag in plain sight on her lapel.

"I don't care if your names are on the list," she snapped, looking them over from head to toe. Nancy suddenly realized how scruffy they all looked. "In fact, I don't care if your names are Rockefeller, Ford, and Getty. Especially you, candy man," she added, glaring at Joe. "You vagabonds will enter this party over my dead body!"

Chapter

Twenty-One

Y OU DON'T UNDERSTAND," Frank said urgently. "This is an emergency!"

"Mm-hm," the guard said. "You'll have an emergency yourself if you don't clear out right now!"

"Excuse me, excuse me," a nimble-footed waiter sang as he walked by. On his right shoulder he was balancing a tray stacked high with steaming plates.

The guard let him by. Then she looked back at Nancy as if she were looking at a child she wanted to spank. "Okay, I'm through playing games with you kids. You're blocking traffic!"

Joe stepped forward to say something, but

before he could, another waiter sped by. "Watch your back! Hot stuff!" he called out.

Nancy pulled Joe's arm. "Come on," she said loudly. "We're just going to have to watch it all on TV."

"But—but—" Joe sputtered.

"Just follow me, everybody," Nancy whispered.

They walked away and turned left down another hallway. Loud voices, cooking smells, and the clatter of china floated out of an open door on their right.

They peeked in and saw cooks and waiters busily preparing food in a bright, white industrial kitchen. Each person was dressed in a crimson-and-white uniform with the insignia of the United Nations.

"Now, they've all got to get their uniforms from *somewhere,*" Nancy said. She hurried down the hallway, testing each door. At last one of them opened up to reveal a large changing room filled with stacks of women's uniforms. "Come on, Bess!" she said.

Down the hall, Frank had found the men's changing room. "Good. There's a shower here," he said. "You can get cleaned up, Joe." He and Joe disappeared inside.

Minutes later they were in the kitchen, stacking salads on big oval trays.

"Put those on tables eight through eleven!" a large, bearded man called out without looking up.

"Right!" Nancy answered. She gave her friends a wink as they headed out the door. "Now remember, hold the tray on your left shoulder and pass the guard on the right side—that way she won't see your face."

The four of them scurried back down the hall. As they got to the security guards' desk, they called out warnings:

"Excuse me! Excuse me!"

"Watch your back!"

"Coming through!"

The guards all stepped aside—or at least Nancy assumed they must have. She couldn't see them.

The din of loud music, shouting voices, and clinking glasses washed over them as they stepped into the room. Nancy put her tray carefully down on a stand next to the table marked 8. She looked around at the room. It was beautiful. Tiny white lights glittered on dozens of miniature pine trees in pots, and candles gleamed in all the windows. But the focal point of the room was a huge glass display case against the wall. Inside were the Sarconne crown jewels they had seen at the museum.

In the middle of the room there was a circular platform surrounded by a high, curved wall of clear Plexiglas. On it, a DJ in a tuxedo was leaning over his electronic equipment. Nancy smiled despite her nervousness. A DJ at this posh party? She knew that must have been Jean-Claude's idea.

There was a dance area around the platform, and beyond that about twenty large, round tables. On each table were eight sterling silver place settings, along with fresh-cut holly, pine boughs, crudités—and an ornate, carved-silver dome near the center.

Nancy reached over to the dome on table 8 and gingerly lifted it. It was just what she'd feared—a chocolate crown-bomb!

"Don't touch!" a heavyset waiter barked at her as she reached for the deadly crown.

Nancy's stomach knotted. What was going to remain of this room—this building!—when all the bombs had been detonated? She exchanged glances with Frank, Joe, and Bess. Here we are, she thought, finally at the party—and all we can do is stand here, completely helpless!

"What are we going to do?" Bess whispered as the four of them huddled together. "Rip out all the detonators?"

"No," Nancy said. "They'd take one look at us and set off the bombs right away."

"Somewhere around here is a transmitter," Joe said. "Only *where?*"

Frank eyed the DJ. "Suspect number one," he said. "I'm going to take a look at his equipment."

As Frank went over to the platform, other waiters scuttled by setting salads down on the tables. Soon the music began to soften, and the DJ's voice boomed over the loudspeakers in a French accent:

"Please take your seats, ladies and gentlemen. I'm told dinner is about to begin. There's been a slight delay in the kitchen, because the chef can't fit all five hundred candles on the birthday cake!"

There was a smattering of laughter as people in tuxedoes and long silk dresses all moved toward their tables and began sitting down.

"I don't see Reynaud," Nancy whispered to Joe.

"I'm not surprised," Joe replied. "You can be sure he doesn't want to be around when the bomb goes off."

Beads of sweat were starting to form on Nancy's forehead. This was getting too close for comfort! She looked around the room for some sort of clue, but all she saw was Frank on his way back from the DJ's platform.

"Not only does that guy have a lousy sense of humor," he complained, "but his equipment is pretty run-of-the-mill stuff—a couple of turntables, an amp, and a sound board—"

The DJ's voice echoed through the room again: "I've also been informed that our guest of honor has arrived. Ladies and gentlemen, please direct your attention to the entrance on my left, and let us rise in a hearty welcome to the Eminent Count Reynaud and the heir to the throne of Sarconne, Crown Prince Jean-Claude!"

"Bravo!" a cry went up. Everyone in the room stood up and faced the archway on the opposite wall as Count Reynaud entered with a big smile.

Then he moved aside and let Jean-Claude step into the archway.

Beaming, Jean-Claude nodded his head to the crowd. His hair was swept back, and his tails draped perfectly over his lean, athletic body.

"Gorgeous," Bess said.

Jean-Claude strode into the room, then stopped. It looked as if Reynaud wouldn't walk with him.

"What's he doing?" Frank asked.

Nancy watched intently. Jean-Claude gestured into the room, but Reynaud shook his head and pointed back out toward the arch. Finally Jean-Claude shrugged and walked toward the platform.

"Reynaud isn't going up with him," Joe said.

"Uh-oh," Frank murmured.

No one else in the room seemed to have noticed anything amiss. To another burst of applause, Jean-Claude stepped up and took the mike from the DJ. With a warm smile and a gentle wave of the hand, he quieted the crowd.

"Did he notice us?" Bess whispered.

"I don't think so," Nancy replied.

"Hello," Jean-Claude said into the mike. "When my father told me about the celebration, he said not to worry; Cousin Reynaud would take care of everything. Well, he was right. But he didn't mention one thing—that Reynaud would make me speak in front of all of you! I really don't know what to say!"

The crowd laughed. A few people shouted encouragement.

"Anyway," Jean-Claude continued, "speaking of my father, I guess I should start by saying he would have liked more than anything else to be right here today. As we all know, he's been looking forward for many years to the official entry of Sarconne to the U.N. . . ."

"He speaks so well," Bess whispered.

"Sssh!" Joe hissed.

"For a long time," Jean-Claude continued, "many of you were opposed to this accord—including my cousin. I know that my father is thrilled and thankful that the difficulties have all been worked out—and that Sarconne can finally enjoy this great opportunity."

This time the applause was like an explosion. Jean-Claude acknowledged the cheering with a red face and a bow. Then he looked to the back of the room and called into the mike, "Did I do all right, Reynaud?"

There was no answer. Nancy looked back to see Reynaud deep in conversation with the DJ. When he realized that Jean-Claude was talking to him, he stepped forward and gave the prince the okay sign. Laughter rippled through the crowd.

Reynaud and the DJ resumed their conversation immediately, and Nancy watched them closely. The DJ's eyes seemed to shift furtively up to the platform and around the room as he listened to the count.

"Do you think what I think?" Frank asked.

Nancy realized that Frank and Joe had been watching the same scene. She nodded. "I think we've got our man," she answered.

The DJ began walking back up to his platform. "Don't let his hands out of your sight," Frank said. He edged close to the platform, followed by Nancy, Joe, and Bess.

"Okay, thank you, Your Highness!" the DJ said, grabbing the mike. Jean-Claude shook his hand, stepped down, and walked to his seat at the center table, just below the platform, as the DJ continued talking. "Now, I'd like to draw your attention to the centerpiece of each table, the pièce de résistance . . ."

He edged backward while he spoke. His free hand groped for something behind him, his eyes darting to Reynaud at the back of the room. Reynaud glared back at him and made a tiny gesture.

The DJ's brow was glistening with sweat. "It was made by special order of the government of Sarconne . . ." he continued.

He stopped at the other side of the platform. There, just inside the Plexiglas barrier, a little metal box was clamped to the side of a sound board—a box with a small switch.

"That's it," Joe murmured. "The circuit connector for the bomb."

"Nancy, I have to get to Jean-Claude!" Bess whispered.

"No, Bess!" Nancy insisted. "Not yet! If they see you now—"

But it was too late. Bess ran across the room toward Jean-Claude, toppling a tray full of dinners.

With a loud clatter, the plates smashed against the ground. Every head in the room turned toward the noise.

Jean-Claude stood up from the head table. "Bess?" he said, bewildered.

In the archway, Reynaud's face was contorted with fury. The DJ looked petrified. "We've got to stop this," Nancy whispered. "Let's go." Nancy, Frank, and Joe moved to the edge of the platform.

Suddenly Reynaud screamed: "Now, you fool! *Now!*"

And with a frantic thrust of his hand, the DJ flicked the switch.

Frank dove under the Plexiglas barrier and grabbed the man's feet. With a startled cry, the DJ fell to the ground.

"You fools!" he hissed, forgetting that the mike was still in his hands. His words boomed out over the speakers. "You'll all be killed in the explosion!"

All at once, hysterical screams sliced the air. "Let me out! Let me out!" a woman next to Nancy babbled. People rushed toward the exits, shoving one another in their desperate hurry. The party had turned into total, terrifying chaos.

"It's too late, Frank! Forget him!" Nancy shouted, trying to pull Frank off the platform.

"No!" Frank answered through gritted teeth. "All he did was open the circuits! We've got to keep him from getting to his radio detonator—"

Yanking his foot out of Frank's hand, the DJ jumped off the platform. As he began running to the rear of the room, he reached into his pocket and pulled out a small radio-size box with an antenna.

"There it is, Frank!" Nancy called.

Frank raced after him. "Oh, no, you don't—" he yelled.

He dove into a flying tackle, grabbing the DJ around the knees. With a shriek the DJ fell to the ground, knocking over a potted Christmas tree. The detonator flew out of his hands and right into the arms of a party guest . . .

Count Reynaud!

Frank scrambled to his feet. Immediately Reynaud turned and fled from the crowd, toward a dark area at a far end of the room. Frank and Joe raced after him.

Nancy looked over her shoulder. "Bess, Jean-Claude! This way!" she shouted.

Ahead of them, Reynaud disappeared behind a red velvet curtain that had been drawn along the far wall.

Frank yanked open the curtain. A few feet inside it, Reynaud stood in an open fire door, his face crimson with rage.

"Take one more step and I'll blow you to bits!"

Reynaud shouted. He was holding his finger over the detonator button.

Joe lunged for him.

"Don't, Joe!" Frank yelled. But it was too late.

Reynaud's eyes burned with fury as Joe leaped toward him. With a single frantic gesture, Reynaud pressed the button.

Chapter

Twenty-Two

D OWN!" FRANK YELLED.

Before Nancy could react, Frank pulled her to the floor. Together they rolled out the door, Jean-Claude and Bess right behind them.

"Get up!" It was Joe's voice.

Nancy looked up in disbelief. Joe was racing down the stairs after Reynaud. "But the bomb—" she began to say.

"Don't worry about that!" Joe yelled. "I clipped the wires near the DJ's platform!"

The sound of a gunshot rang out against the stairwell walls.

"Joe!" Bess cried out. She dashed down the stairs.

"No, Bess!" Jean-Claude tried to grab her hand, but Bess was already halfway to the next landing.

Jean-Claude, Frank, and Nancy took off down the stairs. Past the fourth floor, then the third . . .

"Don't come any farther!" Joe's voice bellowed. They stopped short between the third and second floors.

A few steps below them stood Bess, her hands in the air, her eyes staring down the muzzle of a gun.

A gun clutched by Count Reynaud.

Joe was staring up at them all from the second-floor landing. Beside him were Count Reynaud and the DJ.

Reynaud waved his gun ominously. "I'm sorry it's come to this, Jean-Claude," he said through clenched teeth. "I don't know which one of your worthless friends to finish off first. Although I suppose even killing all of them wouldn't change the fact that months of planning have been completely destroyed."

With a sudden gesture, he stepped up and grabbed Bess's wrist, twisted her around with one hand, and pointed the gun to her head.

"Stay back," he said, "if you want her to remain alive!"

Slowly Reynaud backed down the stairway and made his way into an expansive marble lobby. The DJ walked ahead of him, barking warnings to anyone around.

Nancy, Jean-Claude, Frank, and Joe stood powerless on the stairs.

"Get out of my way!" Reynaud shouted over his shoulder.

Screaming, their faces taut with fear, the crowd of onlookers in the lobby scattered. Behind them, uniformed guards knelt along the periphery and aimed their revolvers at Reynaud.

"Drop the guns and slide them to the center of the floor!" Reynaud ordered, tightening his grip on Bess.

Slowly the guards followed his instructions. The guns made a swishing sound as they slid across the marble floor.

"This is what I like to see," Reynaud said with a sinister grin. "A spirit of international cooperation."

He pulled Bess toward the front door. Suddenly Jean-Claude's voice boomed through the lobby: "No, Reynaud! Stop!"

Reynaud jerked his head as Jean-Claude came running down the last remaining stairs.

"Stop where you are, Jean-Claude!" Reynaud commanded. "*If* you care anything about the life of your opportunistic little girlfriend."

Bess's panic-stricken eyes grew even wider as Jean-Claude slowly advanced on Reynaud from across the lobby. "Please, Reynaud," he begged. "I've always known you as a man who has never hurt anyone. I don't know why you're doing this. Who's forcing you to—"

Something in Reynaud's iron control seemed to snap. "*Forcing* me?" he yelled, his eyes ablaze. "Jean-Claude, how naive of you to believe the underground movement against your father was dead! All these years I have worked so tirelessly to plan our takeover—smoothing out every last detail, plotting this gala tonight—all under complete secrecy."

"Come on," Frank whispered to Joe and Nancy. Reynaud was so caught up in what he was saying that he didn't even notice. As he ranted on, they crouched low and inched their way down behind a wall of people who had gathered along the banister.

Jean-Claude was standing only inches from Reynaud now. Calmly he held out his hand. "Come on, cousin," he said. "You know this will never work. Give me the gun."

When Reynaud spoke, his voice sent an icy chill through the lobby. "Very well, Jean-Claude," he said. "I *will* give it to you."

And with grim intensity, he turned his gun toward Jean-Claude's head.

Without a sound Frank and Joe sprang through the crowd toward him.

"No!" Bess screamed. Desperately she swung her arm upward.

Bang! came the sound of a shot.

"Jean-Claude!" Nancy gasped.

But Jean-Claude was still standing. The bullet had gone into the ceiling.

Nancy rushed forward, but Frank and Joe had already reached Reynaud. With all the strength he had, Frank grabbed Reynaud from behind.

The count staggered backward—and let go of Bess. Joe pulled her away as Frank forced Reynaud to the ground and kicked the gun out of his hand.

Within seconds, Reynaud and Frank had been surrounded by U.N. security guards. Nancy ran toward Bess, but suddenly stopped short. Out of the corner of her eye, she saw the DJ trying to slip out the revolving door.

"Oh, no, you don't!" she said. She raced to the door just as the DJ entered it. He started to push his way through—until Nancy grabbed hold of the next section of the door and pushed the opposite way.

She dug her heels in and angled her body against the door. The DJ was stuck in the glass compartment, inches from escape. "Help me, Joe!" Nancy called out at the top of her lungs. The DJ was pushing, forcing Nancy backward.

But Joe was right behind her. He leaned into the door right beside Nancy and began pushing the other way. Slowly the DJ slid back into the lobby, where a guard slapped handcuffs onto his wrists. Reynaud was also chained to a security guard.

A wave of relief swept through the crowd. Nancy stood still, dazed, as nervous chatter erupted all over the lobby. She watched as Frank and Joe walked out with the guards. She saw Bess in a corner with Jean-Claude, hugging him and sobbing.

With a half-joyful, half-exhausted sigh, Nancy headed outside to help with the police report.

The brisk winter wind sent a chill through Nancy as she watched the police car take away Reynaud and his accomplice. The other four had been picked up, too. She looked into Frank's and Joe's faces and sighed with relief. "It's over!"

"Yes," Jean-Claude said sadly. He looked haggard and depressed. "All this time I was fooled. I should have known not to believe him when he said he supported the U.N. accord." He shook his head. "Who would have suspected Reynaud could deceive us like this?"

"I still don't understand, Jean-Claude," Bess said. "Why did he do it?"

"For years, my cousin was one of the loudest opponents of Sarconne's admission to the U.N. He was active in the opposition party, demanding all sorts of reforms that would weaken the monarchy. Some of the suggestions made sense, but it was revealed by Sarconne intelligence that the party leader had secret plans to overthrow my father. Most of the party members had had no idea of this. When they realized they'd been deceived, the opposition dissolved almost overnight—or so we thought."

"Was the leader ever found?" Nancy asked.

Jean-Claude shook his head gravely. "No. To this day, his identity has remained a mystery."

There was an awkward silence, and then Frank spoke up softly. "I guess the mystery's been solved at last."

"I guess so," Jean-Claude echoed in a choked whisper.

For a few moments no one knew what to say. Nancy looked around nervously, watching the people in the lobby.

Just then her eyes were caught by a couple heading toward the door. She wasn't quite sure what it was about them that was familiar. One of them was a fat man with a gray mustache and wispy gray hair. Next to him was a thin teenage boy with black hair and a rosy, smooth complexion. "Pardon, please," the older man said repeatedly in a heavily accented French voice as the two worked their way through the crowd.

"Strange pair," Joe remarked.

"They sound as if they may be from Sarconne," Jean-Claude said, "but the accent is a little off."

Where have I seen them? Nancy kept asking herself. She took a few steps toward them and looked more closely—closely enough to see a few strands of hair peeking out from around the younger man's collar.

Red hair.

"Fiona!" Nancy blurted. "And that's Dr. Fox!"

Staring straight ahead, the couple suddenly pushed their way out the door. Nancy and her friends tore outside after them, but by the time they got there, the couple had flagged a cab and sped away.

"What's that they dropped?" Frank said, pointing to a small leather duffel bag lying on the sidewalk. He picked it up, peered inside—and gasped. Then he held out the bag so Nancy could see inside.

The bag was full of jewels—the Sarconne jewels that had been on display upstairs.

"I don't believe it," Nancy said, shaking her head. She began to giggle, and the giggle grew into a laugh. "What great detectives. We thwarted the cat burglars after all—and we didn't even know it!"

"Passengers in rows fifteen through twenty-three, please have your boarding passes ready!"

"Well, that's us," Nancy said. She turned to Joe. "Bye! It was—well, it was a trip to remember!"

Joe smiled. "Yeah. I'll never forget the look on Jean-Claude's face when he actually did sign the treaty."

"*I'll* never forget the look on Reynaud's face when they carted him off. He'll have a great Christmas in jail, I'm sure."

Joe laughed and gave Nancy a bear hug. "Bye, Nancy," he said. Then he held his arms out to Bess. "Maybe next time we can get hold of some real chocolate."

"Yeah," Bess said quietly, giving him a quick hug.

Nancy looked up at Frank. What could she say? That it had been fun? That didn't really describe it. That she'd loved working with him? That sounded too official. That he made her feel so wonderful and so *confused* that she couldn't think straight?

None of the above, she decided. Sometimes honesty wasn't the best policy. "Bye, Frank," she said, trying to keep the emotion checked. "Have a wonderful Christmas. I—I, uh, hope we get the chance to do this again."

"Me, too," Frank said.

With a quick wave, Nancy skipped off to the loading gate, where Bess was already showing her pass.

They walked on the plane together and settled into their seats. Bess didn't say a word until the plane left the ground. Then she burst into tears.

"He—he told me his trip taught him about *responsibility!*" She wept. "He's going to stay in Sarconne and learn to become a good leader."

"That sounds wonderful, Bess," Nancy said.

Bess nodded. "I know. That's the problem. Everything about him is wonderful. Except for the fact that I'll probably never see him again, unless he decides to have an international conference in River Heights."

She blew her nose and reached down under the seat to pull out a bag of chocolate-chip cookies from her shoulder bag. She took a large bite of one and began to munch as she looked sadly out the window. "All I can say is, *you* know how to do it right, Nancy. You never get involved."

Nancy nodded. Bess was right about that. At least this time, anyway.